A Healing Heart

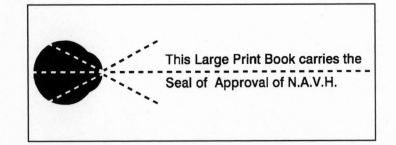

This Large Print Book carries the
Seal of Approval of N.A.V.H.

A HEALING HEART

ANGELA BREIDENBACH

THORNDIKE PRESS
A part of Gale, Cengage Learning

GALE
CENGAGE Learning·

Detroit • New York • San Francisco • New Haven, Conn • Waterville, Maine • London

GALE
CENGAGE Learning®

LIBRARY OF CONGRESS CATALOGING-IN-PUBLICATION DATA

Breidenbach, Angela.
  A Healing Heart : Quilts of Love Series / By Angela Breidenbach. — Large Print edition.
    pages cm. — (Quilts of Love Series) (Thorndike Press Large Print Clean Reads)
    ISBN 978-1-4104-6458-3 (hardcover) — ISBN 1-4104-6458-X (hardcover) 1. Quilts—Fiction. 2. Quiltmakers—Fiction. 3. Man-woman relationships—Fiction. 4. Large type books. I. Title.
PS3602.R445H43 2014
813'.6—dc23   2013037530

Published in 2014 by arrangement with Abingdon Press.

Printed in the United States of America
1 2 3 4 5 6 7 18 17 16 15 14

To my husband, Mike
Thank you for the moment of
brilliance that sparked the
fascinating conversation where
A Healing Heart *was born.*

ACKNOWLEDGMENTS

A Healing Heart wouldn't have come to be without the team of people in my life. I write today with appreciation for those lovely souls willing to help answer questions in my research and those who offered love, hope, and support through the challenge of writing a novel when real life happens. Thank you:

Michael Gill, marketing manager at Bridg erBowl.com who helped me choose a location for avalanches and snowmobiling. Visit Bridger Bowl near Bozeman for all sorts of snow sports!

Museum of the Rockies, thank you for your information about the Museum Ball.

Pam Morris and Rachel Morgan thank you for your patience in letting me read out loud to you for so long and for your fantastic friendship, feedback, and critiques! Julie Cowan my awesome supportive friend who encourages me constantly and is a great beta reader. Lisa Weber for your constant prayers over the phone after the car accident happened in the middle of my deadline race. Vickie Kammerer, beta reader extraordinaire. Yes, I did rename the hospital social worker after you! Thank you for answering my hospital questions.

Prayer supporters and critique friends Rachel Neal, MT Pages, Montana Romance Writers, Advanced Writers and Speakers Association (AWSA), Finish-the-Book-Loop of FHL/RWA chapter, and the Christian Authors Network (CAN) are a major part of my writing life. I'm so glad you're there for me!

My husband, Mike, thank you for your snow cave, Boy Scout info, and brainstorming support at the oddest moments. Speaking of family, thanks Devan and Katie for answering a lot of "life in Bozeman" questions up to the last weekend of deadline. My dad, Al Bigelow, for telling me I can do anything I set my mind to. My stepmom, Wanda Wallace, for starting the tradition of photo memory quilts in our family. You've created an amazing legacy of love in quilt art.

To those authors who made time in their busy lives to read and endorse my first novel, I am forever grateful. I know how hard it is to carve out time on deadlines now. Your words are emblazoned on my heart. Thank you so much for encouraging me to continue in my career dreams through your endorsements.

My agent, Tamela Hancock Murray of the Steve Laube Agency; Ramona Richards, my Quilts of Love editor; and the Abingdon Press team for the opportunity to discover this story from a simple paragraph idea. I'll always have the best "how did your first novel happen" story!

From a heart overflowing in gratitude,
Angie

1

Why in the world did I agree to do this?

Mara Keegan's vision blurred as she stared at the old photo she'd picked from the box for the first block on Cadence's memory quilt. David's arm curled tightly around her pregnant waist, his other balanced a precocious three-year-old Cadence, and one-year-old Toby grinned up into his mommy's eyes. Louie, the new family border collie/lab pup sat at their feet ready to catch Toby's graham cracker.

A smile stole across Mara's lips. Louie nabbed that cracker and Toby wailed, right after the shutter clicked. But the picture captured the split-second happy moment forever. The perfect family with so much promise. A promise broken off prematurely by a whimsical God.

Mara's smile faded. She glanced over at her sleeping fourteen-year-old dog curled up on one of his favorite oversized mutt mats. He'd been with their family since the early days. His black muzzle sported more white around his nose now. Louie seemed like the bridge from past to present as she looked back at the first picture. When would she be ready to try love again? Did she even need it? She broke out in a sweat in spite of the cold wind blowing the last of December past her windows. Not until she could trust God again. How could it have all gone so wrong? The wind gust whooshed against her office door and rattled the inset glass.

A burning sensation started in the center of Mara's chest. She wrapped her ankles around the wooden stool legs and anchored her feet as she rubbed her midsection. This gift was taking more out of her than she had expected. With less than five months to Cadence's graduation, she had to design and create a quilt full of memories. Memories Cadence needed as she left for college. Memories to wrap around her when she felt far from home and family. Memories Mara promised Cadence, and Mara never broke a promise.

Mara dug in her purse for a chewable antacid tablet. They'd become her favorite candy the last few months. Especially today, since the official documents for the new contract were lost when her computer network crashed after the big windstorm tore down power lines last night. No one had had power for the last twelve hours on this side of Bozeman. This government contract could change the future of her business and the community. But her business mentor, Rich, jumped in to help. He'd kept the e-mails. By the time the computers blinked on this afternoon, she'd have his advised changes and be able to print out another set, postmark a hard copy, and fax the acceptance before the close of business back East. Okay, maybe she should eat a little better. She popped a tablet in her mouth, scowled at the mini bottle, and threw it back in her purse.

The box of photos held too many memories. To choose the right ones for Cadence, Mara needed to sort through them one by one. "Why didn't I just buy Cadence a car, huh, Louie?" Something easy that didn't rip her heart out every minute of the planning. The dog opened his eyes and cocked an ear at her. The burn radiated out further. She pressed hard against her stomach to ease the pain. The antacid should help soon.

She should have eaten more than a skim latte for lunch. She needed an early start on all the photos for the T-shirt transfers. Once the photos finished printing out on transfer paper, she could leave them with Tina at the T-shirt shop overnight and pick up the photos pressed onto the poplin tomorrow. Nausea built until it reached the middle of Mara's chest and wallowed there, squeezing the little bits of heart she had left. It figured she'd have the beginnings of an ulcer. Her neck muscles tensed and sent a shooting pain into her jaw. She opened and closed her jaw joint and wiggled the bones of her chin, but the motion didn't soothe the tension.

How long could she go on living with the way things turned out? The stress from carrying the entire business load left her with this constant tension and now the heartburn. Mara rolled her head from shoulder to chest to opposite shoulder. David's snowmobiling accident left her in charge of twenty-five employees, business loans, and a dream built for two. But now there was one. Three years from the moment the snow buried him in the avalanche. Three years since David breathed his last. And she hadn't stopped to breathe since. She hated the week after Christmas since the accident. Sacrilegious or not, she hated it.

Mara shook her head to clear the pity party. So a little more lost sleep, what's new? The sooner she plowed into this promise, the sooner she'd get the sleep she needed. This present would be done on time if it was the last thing she did. Breaking the family tradition, a quilt for graduation, was not an option. It meant too much to Cadence. Maybe Mara should switch out the lavender candle for a citrus scent and wake up her brain. She looked up at it. Maybe later. She inhaled the calm fragrance.

Her head pounded. The caffeine seemed to create more jitters than normal. She pushed away the remaining drink. It'd gone cold anyway. She pulled the hair band out of her high ponytail to loosen the tension on her scalp. Mara massaged tender spots under her thick mane with one hand while she spread out several photo choices on the white work space. Maybe she should consider cutting off several inches. The weight alone might cause these headaches. But David had always loved her hair. She hadn't cut it more than to shape it in longer than she could remember. Had she even done that this year? Her hair was always in an updo for business, so no one saw the condition it was in. She swept up the ends of her hip-length burnished brown locks and grimaced at them. Maybe a little change would do her good. Yeah, right. When was that going to happen? She picked up the family photo again unable to let it go. Change wasn't always good.

Mara's heart twisted, radiating out searing pain. She slapped a hand out for balance and instead flipped the box of photos over as she tumbled off the work stool onto the cold floor. The wooden chair clanged to the rustic clay tiles with her legs tangled in the chair rungs. The box rained down life-moment scenes as if a movie reel unwound in front of her eyes. Her son, Toby, at T-ball, Marisa's Disney Princess birthday party, and Cadence with her younger siblings tackling their daddy. Was she having a heart attack?

Louie barked in surprise and jumped up from his massive plaid dog pillow.

Pictures fluttered and scattered across the floor.

Mara's hand held fast to her family forever frozen in a joyful pose — before God pulled his whimsical trick.

Louie barked again and bounded across the room, sliding on slick paper, to stick his nose into the back of Mara's neck. He lay down with his muzzle across her right shoulder buried in her long brown hair.

Mara blinked. What just happened? Oh, there. She focused on David. His strong face, his tanned muscular arms that held

her close, and those sparkling brown eyes grinning with little crinkles she used to trace with her fingers. David, David, I miss you. She closed her eyes.

Mara Keegan. Joel sighed as he tucked the file under his arm. Would she remember? Would she throw him out? As he rang the doorbell, Joel heard a dog barking inside. Then a pretty teen with unusual golden coloring flung the front door wide.

"Louie, knock it off!" She yelled toward the back of the house. "Sorry, he's kind of protective. Can I help you?"

"Hi, I'm Joel Ryan," he stuck out his hand. "Here to consult with Mara Keegan on the government contract. Is she here?"

"Sure. I'm Cadence, her daughter." She invited him in and shivered as she flicked the ornate door closed. "Cold out there, huh?"

"Well, it's sure not as warm as my last consulting visit in California." Joel smiled. "But I'm used to it. I'm from Colorado."

She had a slight Native American look, but her hair was a reddish-brown and dark freckles dotted her golden cheeks. Her eyes were almost rust and rimmed with long black lashes. She wore very little makeup.

Joel wondered about her mother, the

17

woman he had yet to meet in person. Only a phone call five years ago, but now he hoped Mara didn't remember him. He swallowed. That wasn't one of his finer moments. Better to get it out of the way if she did put two and two together. By God's grace, he was a different person now. Would Mara have the grace to forgive?

Louie barked several more times. "Louie, that's enough!" Cadence yelled again. "I don't know what's up with him. He quits as soon as the doorbell does, but he's usually here all up in your face and checking you out, too." She looked around for the dog. "Weird."

"Nice Christmas tree." Joel nodded at the decorated fake evergreen to be polite. It was a nicer tree than the miniature tree on his coffee table, all designer perfect. The red and green plaid ribbons on his tree looked as if someone had tied each one exactly the same. His tree barely had lights.

Cadence gave the tree a small glance. "Yeah, thanks."

He checked his triple-time-zone watch. His favorite tool never disappointed. Travel and daily contact with clients from Pacific to Mountain to Eastern kept him in a constant chase of the correct time. Clients in any part of the country could count on

his prompt call or arrival. Plenty of time to meet the deadline, but there was no sense in delay. "May I meet with Mara?"

"Sure, follow me. She's back in her workroom." A hint of resentment floated in her tone. "Like always."

The TV screen held a frozen Wii game with several cartoon Wii avatars. "Mom" wore a purple shirt and long dark hair. He sidestepped the Wii balance board on the floor and followed.

"There's another entrance for that part of the house, if you want to use it next time." Cadence traipsed off into a long hallway with her braid swinging.

"Mom!" Cadence rounded the corner.

Mara lay on her left side, stiff and chilled. She opened her eyes at the alarm in her daughter's voice.

Cadence knelt at Mara's feet, gently picked up her mom's top ankle, and unthreaded the wooden stool from Mara's legs.

"I'm okay —" Mara tried to sit up but only made it to her elbow. She didn't have the strength to push up all the way past the sharp pain in her shoulder. The dizziness rushed back. Her whole body didn't feel all that great now either since hitting the floor. But her left shoulder really ached all the

19

way on the inside — wow!

"Cadence, is everything all right?" A man stood in the doorway. He wore a dark blue ski parka over a business suit. Louie growled as the hair along his backbone stood on end. He leaped and stood over Mara. The man jumped back into the hall away from the big dog.

"No, Louie, no!" Cadence kept her voice steady but firm. "Joel, he's not mean," she said without looking away from her mother. She moved around to Mara's back and pulled Louie aside by his collar. "Good boy, now go lie down."

Mara glanced at the stranger near the door. He looked ready to take over, but Louie held him at bay. Her old dog stood on guard, disregarding Cadence's command.

"Here, I'll help you up." With her arm around Mara's back, Cadence tried to lift her.

"I don't think I can stand yet." Mara leaned against the table leg. "Just give me a minute to catch my breath." She shivered at the cold seeping up from the tiles into her legs. The shiver started a new spasm of pain in her shoulder and ankle.

"Sheesh, Mom, what did you do? How'd you end up on the floor?" Cadence still knelt beside Mara and waited.

"I don't know." Mara gasped for air. "One minute I was picking out pictures for your quilt and the next I fell. Maybe I have the flu. I'm a little light-headed." She pressed her stomach and fought for control of the nausea. "I might have twisted my ankle, though. Man, it hurts!" She wanted to reach for her left leg, but the pain in her shoulders held her back.

"Louie." Cadence pointed at the dog bed. "Go!" Louie crept backward an inch at a time fighting his instinct to protect. His long ears stayed flattened back on his gleaming black head and his eyes trained on Joel without a flinch.

Joel eyed Louie and stepped into the room. "May I suggest we get you checked out?"

Mara dragged in another breath. "Who are you?" Her lips trembled and her heart fluttered out of control.

"I'm Joel, your new consultant from Business Mentors, Inc. I'm replacing Rich." He put a file down on her worktable. "I really think we ought to get you to the ER." He moved closer toward Mara and knelt down at her level.

"I don't need —"

"Mom, you don't look good at all. I think

he's right. You're like, white as your shirt."

But she could ask the doctor to check her heart. No, that's silly. At thirty-nine, she probably just had a bad case of the flu. Mara's arm throbbed with sharp jabs, her neck and jaw muscles clenched tight. She'd probably sprained her shoulder now, too.

Exhausted she bit out, "Fine, fine. I probably need an antibiotic or something." Another shiver shot through her. "I'm sure it's the flu. I have the chills and I ache all over." Mara rubbed her left arm.

Joel moved in to Mara's side to help her stand. Together both Cadence and Joel lifted Mara from the floor.

"Ow, ow! I can't —" Mara felt herself swing up. Her head lolled back from the motion.

"I've got you. You can trust me." He glanced over at her daughter. "Cadence, would you grab a blanket for her and let's go." Joel tipped his head toward the door. "We'll take my car so you can help your mom if she needs it."

"I don't need —"

"Really?" Joel's blue eyes captured hers again. "Can you walk?"

A shooting pain screeched through her left side.

2

"Well, Mrs. Keegan, your blood pressure is up. That's common with pain, though. Your test results don't show any markers for concern beyond taking care of your injuries." The doctor flicked a light in and out of her eyes. "I remember how hard it was for you losing your husband. That was an awful accident." He listened to her chest. "The dizziness you experienced, have you had that before?"

Mara shook her head no. "I skipped lunch and just had a double latte."

The doctor looked at her with disapproval. "That could be the cause of the heart racing you felt. I'm not hearing it now though." He wrapped the stethoscope around his neck. "It appears you're experiencing some stress and panic attacks. We see this kind of thing sometimes around the anniversary of losing loved ones, especially during the holidays. You've got it all going on right now, don't you?"

She didn't want to think about David's time in the hospital. The sight of his mangled body and skin scraped raw seared into her mind. She'd had no appetite then either. Three years and the traumatic scene still affected whether she ate or not. "I should have eaten lunch. I just couldn't handle it today."

"No more skipping lunch. We don't need any more fainting spells." He took another look at her shoulder. "You're going to have a sore left shoulder from your fall for a few days but I think it'll be fine. Just a little bruising. You might consider seeing a chiropractor."

He moved to the counter and picked up her chart. As he made notes he added, "It's good you're building a new life." The doctor gestured at Joel with his pen.

"New life?" Mara realized he meant Joel, who'd carried her into the hospital and never left her side. She let out an involuntary groan.

The doctor didn't acknowledge her question. "You can't keep going at the pace you are and not expect some kickback. I'm going to refer you to a counselor for stress reduction."

"A counselor." Mara gripped the side of

the ER bed and willed herself into stillness. He'd said it with nonchalance. She chose not to make eye contact with anyone else in the room, especially not Joel.

The doctor patted her hand. "It's common, don't worry." The doctor finished marking up her chart.

Mara pulled her hand away and rubbed her temple. *Counselor, my foot!*

"I'm also going to suggest you take a stronger antacid for indigestion in a daily dose. If you'll follow the directions for an acid-reducing diet, I think it'll help your appetite by removing the irritants to your system. You could stand to gain a few pounds for your health." He turned to the laptop on the counter. "Then if you'll take a good hard look at your schedule, you do need to lower your stress before you really have a heart attack." He looked over at Joel, "She needs some rest and TLC."

Joel nodded. "I'll see what I can do."

Mara broke in. "No, I don't need him to —" She stopped talking at the doctor's raised eyebrows. He handed her a printout of a prescription. "Fine, fine." She clamped her lips together and breathed in slow, even breaths.

"Now we know your heart is okay, let's see what those X-rays say about that ankle . . ."

Mara sat still trying hard not to wince. Could it get any worse? But the tech assigned to casting her broken ankle didn't seem any too gentle. Some men didn't know their own strength. She snuck a look at Joel. Okay, he'd been gentle and careful as he carried her into the hospital. She'd give him that.

Joel appeared intent to stay and help her through the entire contract process. To be fair, where else would he go and what else would he do? He'd flown into Bozeman to help her and to build the new team. His two-day visit would check for any missed details in her business plan. Production needed to start right after New Year's. Could it get any worse? He'd carried her out of her house, into the ER, and now he planned to sit with her through the casting.

If she were ready to notice men again, he was very handsome, too. Blue eyes, light brown hair, and smile lines accented his sympathetic grin. Would it be cowardly to crawl under the exam table? Mara released the breath she'd been holding. It wouldn't matter anyway. The doctor just said she was stressed out and unstable. This man looked like he could have his pick of stable, rational women. *Oh, that's professional. Think work.*

That's where my focus has to be. "Well, at least I can sit at my desk."

"Mom, seriously, you have to take some time off. The doctor said no weight on your foot for two weeks."

"I'd be bored spitless. What am I supposed to do sitting around all day?"

A nurse popped in with a paper cup of water and a pill.

"What's this?"

"The doctor sent you a prescription-strength dose of ibuprofen until you can get your prescription for the pain meds filled. It'll help with the swelling." The nurse handed her the paper cup.

She chased the bitter horse pill with one gulp of the water. Mara handed the minuscule cup back. The nurse stepped out and closed the curtain.

"You could work on my quilt, and I could take care of you."

Cadence's face showed so much compassion and hope that Mara wanted nothing more than to spend time with her. But who'd do the payroll, pay the bills, and approve material orders, let alone double-check the designs and quality control? The plant employees were excellent, but always needed a guiding hand. She'd caught an error on the last pack design that would have sewn two pockets together on the inside during assembly. How would that look to ski rescue teams when they couldn't store gear properly? No, she'd be dependable because she'd had to be for the last three years.

She'd made David a promise in this same hospital that she'd see their dream through, and in doing so she'd become indispensable to twenty-five employees who supported almost that many families. Orders came from local ski shops and regional rescue teams. The bid from the government would take her business to national, if not international, recognition.

"Cadence, you know better. Too many people count on me. People with families to feed. I can't just fall down on the job because I have a boo-boo."

Cold. Cadence copped a cold mask. One all too familiar the last few years. Mara held her sigh, her feelings of failure rising inside. Cadence might understand someday when she became a mother. *Oh, I hope she never has to understand failing her children.*

Joel sputtered, "I'd say you already did."

Cadence's eyes twinkled. Then she couldn't hold the giggle back. "Yep, he's got ya. Besides a busted ankle isn't a boo-boo. It's a major injury." She folded her arms with an I-told-you-so glint.

Mara gritted her teeth. "Okay." She then sent a look heavenward as the tech lifted her foot. She fought not to groan out the words. "Fine, fine."

Joel had the courtesy to turn away to smile. "I do have one thing that needs your signature immediately." He turned back, the glimmer still in his eyes.

Mara's face blanched. "The contract!" How could she have forgotten she needed to sign something as important as a government contract that would double her employee base in this economy? Her business had to grow or die. People relied on her. Families relied on her ability to provide jobs in the community. She had dozens and dozens of applicants waiting to hear whether they'd get a job or go to the food bank again. Wives trying to supplement while husbands were laid off, single moms who finally had a way to work while kids were in school, even a machine tech to keep her equipment repairs in-house. Her leg hurt something ferocious, but the pain paled against the hopeful faces seared into her mind.

"Let's get it done right away." She sucked air through her teeth. Her Crow and Irish ancestors must have endured much more.

She could manage because breaking a promise would be a good deal more painful than breaking an ankle. An ankle heals. A broken promise festered for a lifetime and could destroy lives, families. She knew. David had broken his promise to spend his life with her and God let him.

"Mrs. Keegan, I need you to sit still."

Another man telling her what to do. Again. Mara bristled. "There are people I've been interviewing for weeks. I cannot let them down. I have two dozen —"

"No problem if we can get you back to your house to fax it before the end of day, Eastern Standard Time. Then I can get the original postmarked and sent off." Joel looked at his watch. "That means we still have about an hour since it's only two here."

The tech shook his head. "I'm sorry, but you'll be here for at least that long."

"An hour?" Was David shaking his head at her up in heaven? "Okay, now I think I'm going to throw up." She should have thought to check if her network was back online before leaving home or at least called her assistant to do the checking. "I didn't get the notes from Rich on the contract yet with the power outage. It's not at my house. I just ran home on lunch to get the photos picked out for Cadence's quilt. I planned on dropping them off to have them ironed onto the quilt squares." Her head snapped up. "How did you know where I lived, and what were you doing there rather than at the office?"

"I called when I landed to get directions out to the shop. Your assistant, Jill, sent me to your home office. Since time is critical, I brought the contract you e-mailed Rich to go over with you. I have the notes he wrote into it for the changes."

Jill, the fast thinker, always kept up with Mara's schedule. She knew how important this opportunity would be for everyone. Mara made a mental note to praise Jill for her foresight. It wasn't her fault the broken ankle caused the delay. She may have saved the contract, too.

"I'm glad she did. I, well, I really appreciate how helpful you've been," Mara said.

Joel nodded. "I'm glad I could help." He ducked his head, "But I left it on the worktable at your house."

"My house! Why didn't you say so?" Mara started to twist toward Joel. "Holy cow, now what?"

The tech put a large forearm across Mara's knees anchoring her in place. "Ma'am, I'm afraid you are going to have to sit still or I can't wrap your foot."

Would screaming in the emergency room be out of the ordinary? Probably wouldn't win her any points. She didn't need the extra attention either. "Fine, fine." She took a deep, controlled breath of the disinfectant-scented air. Her heart thumped unevenly. How did one go about lessening stress if deep breathing didn't do it? She breathed in slower, deeper, and willed away the swell of panic. *See? No counselor needed.*

"Mara, we've been a little preoccupied the last few hours." Joel swept both hands up and gestured at her and around the facility with his hands. "Someone has a broken ankle."

He must be Italian or something. He seemed to talk with his hands a lot. The government didn't care about her broken ankle. Mara asked, "How much longer will this *really* take?"

The attendant gave her an icy stare, "About an hour." He pulled the silver cart closer.

Revise that. The government didn't care about her ankle, and the attendant didn't care about her contract. Could it get any more ironic? "We'll never make it. My house is fifteen minutes away."

"I'll go get it."

She scooted him out with her hands. "Go, go!"

He stood up from the hard hospital chair. "I'm on it." Joel spun toward the exit. He stopped. "Cadence, do you think you could grab a sandwich or something for your mom?"

"Joel!"

Cadence clapped her hand over her mouth to hide the giggle as Joel slung the curtain open and closed.

3

Mara's iPhone vibrated in Joel's pocket as he dashed through the hospital halls to the rental car. Cadence passed it to him when she'd gone with her mom to X-ray. A quick look around, and he pulled it out of his pocket. Caller ID flashed a government number. He knew he had to take it for Mara. "Bridger Pack and Rescue, Joel speaking."

"Excuse me, I thought I called Mara Keegan." The woman responded.

"Yes, you did. I'm monitoring her cell at the moment while she's in an important appointment." The complete truth. There wasn't any more important appointment in Mara's life right now than casting her leg. *Lord, please help her heal quickly.* The only one who didn't realize Joel had her phone was Mara.

The caller launched into the demand for a finalized contract. "I've been waiting for the signature fax on our contract. Where is it?"

"I'm aware of the situation. How can I help you?" Frigid air blasted through the automatic hospital door as he ran toward the parking lot. He jogged with carefully placed steps across the patchy ice.

Irritation spouted through the airwaves. "I need that signed document in my hands before the close of day or we'll award the contract to the next applicant."

"We've had a slight delay, but should be on track shortly." No one needed to know Mara's private concerns, especially not a government employee with a waiting list of other competing contract bids. "Can you give me another hour or two?"

"Deadlines are deadlines," she stated in monotone. "I'm not waiting past five. We're on cutbacks, not overtime. Do you under-stand?"

"Yes, completely. You'll have it." The phone went dead. Someone was having a bad day. Okay, maybe bad days were conta-gious. *Lord, a little help here please. There are a lot of people counting on this op-portunity. Please help move any delays out of my way.* Joel pulled out of the parking lot. His prayers were answered as red lights flashed to green as soon as he approached.

Then came Louie. Adrenaline zinged through Joel's veins as he stared through the engraved oval glass at the big guard dog. He hadn't thought about the dog. But the dog definitely thought about Joel as he stood on guard inside Mara's office. Louie's growl came through the door's oval glass loud and clear. Joel could see the file on the opposite side of the massive worktable. He checked his watch for the hundredth time. Forty-five minutes left. *Think man!* Dog attacks, no file. What if he went to the front door, rang the bell, and then quietly snuck back to the side of the house. He might have enough time to run in, slam the inside office door shut, grab the file, and get out. It was worth a try.

"Hey, you! What are you doing?"

Joel looked around. The voice seemed to come from closer to the front yard.

A woman's voice on the other side of the fence hollered. "Who are you?"

He spotted a short, older woman at the end of the yard and called back. "I'm a friend." It dawned on him the neighbor might help him with the dog. "Mara's broken her ankle. She sent me for a file on her desk, but Louie's not about to let me in. Do you know him? Can you help me?"

"Hang on. I've heard of scammers like

you. You crooks get old folks like me to give money to help our stranded friends or grandchildren out of some foreign country."

A minute later, a gray-haired woman came slowly around the side of the house with a wheeled walker. "Who did you say you are?" She peered up at him with a scrunched nose and squinted eyes. Her glasses slipped off her nose and fell against her chest dangling from a beaded chain. "Oh, poo." She put them back on.

He smiled. She needed to trust him. Joel summoned intense control not to rush her. "I'm Joel, Mara's new business coach."

"How do I know you're telling the truth? Mara sure doesn't need any more heartache right about now. She's a busy, busy gal with enough worries." She studied him closely.

"No, ma'am. Please, she's about to lose a government contract if I can't get her signature and get it faxed before end of day on the East Coast. Then she will have more worries." Joel pointed at the elusive paperwork. "You can see the file right there through the glass." Seconds ticked away as the white-haired, self-ordained Neighborhood Watch considered his story and looked him over top to toe. He held his ground.

"Hmm, I don't think you'd lie about something like that, would you, young man?" The lady tapped a finger against her chin. "Our Mara sure is good for Bozeman. Yes, she is. She's got a good company she and her David were building. Now she's still putting people back to work. You know she went from just the two of them to over twenty-five employees in two years. And she's kept it going all by her lonesome. Good woman. She works too hard though, being a mom and all that. She needs to be home with her children more. And I do wish she could get back to her designing —"

"Please." Joel smiled again to take the sting out of his interruption. "Can you help with Louie?"

"Oh, sure I can." She opened the door. A rush of lavender scent from the still burning candle greeted them. "Louie, good boy. Let's go for a walk." At the word "walk," Louie's ears perked up and if a dog could dance a jig, he did. His feet pranced in place while his whole body vibrated as if to bagpipes. His tail thumped the wood on the lower part of the door like a bass marching drum. Shoot, he didn't need bagpipes. The excited dog was his own parade.

"I watch him when Mara and the kids visit family. More like he watches me." The spry grandma laughed at her own joke. "He walks me around the block every day so I get the exercise my doctor says I need. Never leaves me. He just glues himself right here to my side." She chuckled again and leaned a hand out. Louie ran up to her and snuggled into her leg. He stuck his nose into her hand and nudged for cherished strokes.

"Thank you, Mrs. — I'm sorry?" Joel's relief warred with his need to be polite and a little concern over the old woman's balance with the big dog.

"Calder. I'm Miriam Calder."

"Mrs. Calder. Thank you. I'll get that file and get on back to the hospital." He dashed inside, grabbed the file, and made a quick check to see that the contract pages and notes were still in it. Joel blew out the candle and dashed back out.

"What did you say happened to our Mara?" Mrs. Calder reached over to close the door.

"She fell and broke an ankle earlier. She's getting a cast right now." He checked the time. "I've really got to run." Thirty-six minutes left and a fifteen-minute drive he somehow needed to cut by several minutes.

"Now how did she do that? Oh, my!" Mrs. Calder looked worried.

Joel stopped himself from turning away. "Seems she fainted and fell off her stool there from skipping lunch."

"I knew it, I knew it. She doesn't take good enough care of herself. Everyone else sure, but she lets herself go without." Mrs. Calder clucked her tongue. "Well, I'll get a little something together to feed the family. It's the least I can do for all they do for me." The dog pranced around the elderly lady in a circle. His attention never left her face. "Louie-boy, looks like we need a little meander before we cook up something nice. Let's walk." He fell into an obedient heel.

Joel took the chance and hightailed it to the car. A momentary worry tugged at him for Mrs. Calder's welfare. He glanced backward in his mirror and smiled. Louie hadn't even cared he was there once Mrs. Calder showed up. The old woman moved at a pretty quick clip with that walker and the big black dog with his white tuxedo chest paced himself at a perfect match to her speed. Joel assured himself she'd be okay and pulled away from the curb. He'd have to remember the magic word — walk.

Joel couldn't remember a time he'd felt more alive since running his own company. Two minutes to spare on the return trip, thanks to Mara and Cadence watching from inside the hospital door. They helped Mara into the car in record time.

Joel raced to the nearby copy shop for the fax and mail service. He rushed in, sent them off, then snapped a quick photo of the documents and attached them to an e-mail. Better safe than sorry. He sent the e-mail to the government employee via Mara's iPhone as proof of the fax and time. Either one should be sufficient, but Mara had additional proof with the documents in her e-mail with a time stamp in case the fax on the other end failed to print. The copy shop also helped with the mail service. This time they'd have a tracking number.

Deadlines invigorated Joel. The challenge to make the impossible happen sang through his blood as he left the shop. Maybe he shouldn't have sold his business. He missed the everyday tension. But he had to admit helping another to succeed was very rewarding. *Maybe success was sweeter when there was someone to share it with.* That must be why coaching appealed to him now. He loved the sense of celebration he could share with clients.

He flung the car door open and grinned. "We made it, Mara." His rental car held the faint scent of lavender that seemed to float around Mara. He liked it. A lot. The famous Montana painter, Charles Russell, couldn't have found a more perfect native woman

41

for his model. So why was she looking at him like she didn't trust him? Had two and two equaled four already? Didn't this afternoon count for anything?

Her hazel eyes looked him over while she chewed on her lower lip.

The closer he was physically to Mara, the easier he could see how long dark lashes emphasized the distinct mahogany star rimmed by the olive green in her eyes. A shiver ran down his spine that had nothing to do with the weather as he took in her exotic features.

The fact she was Native American, if only a quarter, and a female business owner, gave her the extra points in the bidding system to win the contract against other equal bids. But it wasn't something she'd used before even for business loans. Joel didn't know if she was aware Rich altered the contract for the benefit of the minority opportunities. It was a change they were supposed to go over before Mara signed. They'd still have to go over it, but first she needed to agree to his coaching. Then he had the distinct feeling the minor contract change would be another challenge with Mara.

"Joel." Her voice held caution. "I never heard your last name. Joel what?"

Here it comes. She'd know immediately.

He swallowed and slid into the driver's seat. "Joel Ryan." He kept his eyes on the dashboard. He didn't want to see the ugly result of his name cross her beautiful face. *God? This was your idea and it's feeling more like I'm on the ice in Antarctica.*

"Joel Ryan?" She squeaked. They'd had no contact in over five years. All she knew of him was the old slimy lizard who tried one time too many to buy out the fledgling company because he saw quick money. All communication had been via mail or legal counsel.

"You've got to be kidding me. What did you do, sneak up here to trick me? Did you change something in the contract I didn't catch?"

"Hold on there. I'm not the one who lost the documents." He held up a hand. "I'm your new business coach. For me to be successful, you have to be successful. I didn't change anything in the contract after you signed it, and I'm not going to take advantage of you."

"Why would you be different now?" Hope that she'd be okay with the new business coach Rich sent her dimmed like the dark clouds overhead as they rolled in heavy with the next snowstorm. The sky darkened further as the sun flipped its switch and sank behind the buildings of downtown Bozeman. *Big sky, my foot.* She couldn't see one bit of it past the massive low system. The snow hit hard. Wind whipped white flurries across the hood. Not even the Bridger Mountains were visible.

"Mara, let's get you back home. Then we can talk."

"I don't think so. I think we talk now." Mara pulled the blanket closer as she crossed her arms. "What are *you* doing here?"

Joel turned on the engine to warm up the interior as the snow billowed around them. The gusts rocked the SUV.

Joel swallowed, "Rich Katella's load was evaluated and redistributed so you'd get better coaching into the future as he prepares to retire."

"How am I going to get better coaching from the man who tried to steal my company?"

"Mom?" Cadence's voice carried over the SUV seatback.

"What?" Mara snapped. Her breath fogged into the air, freezing like her attitude.

Joel glanced in the rearview mirror.

Mara realized her mistake. She closed her eyes for a split second to gather her emotions and then turned around.

Cadence's face drew into an unemotional mask, but she didn't back down. "Joel is the one who helped us today. Could you let him explain?"

"Fine, fine." Mara looked back at Joel and lifted her brows in expectation. She plastered on what she hoped was a neutral expression. She didn't know if she'd forgive and forget, but she had to try and at least listen for Cadence's sake.

"I sold my company a few years back. I wasn't ready to retire at thirty-eight. So when the company that coached me to success approached me, I accepted a position. I don't buy out companies any more for my catalog business. I help people grow their companies instead."

"Changing jobs doesn't make any difference. Your ethics are still the issue." Mara faced the windshield where gathering snow built an icy wall like the wall around her heart. Could he change from the ruthless businessman who'd tried to devour the hard work of others? He'd carried her into the hospital. Could she forget he'd nearly destroyed the business and her family's financial health? She protected her company, her people, as if they were her tribe and not mere employees.

"No, you're right. My ethics were the issue. In fact, Rich was my coach, too. He took me to task for questionable behavior, and it was his example that made me want to do business the right way."

"What do you mean?"

"Rich showed me how to change my business practices for a more successful and profitable company," Joel said. "But he also showed me how to live a more successful life."

The warm air started to thaw Mara as she studied Joel. She wanted to believe him, but life taught her those with good intentions often didn't follow through. "Well, you'll have to prove that to me."

He turned to face Mara. "Rich helped me understand what success really is and what it isn't. It's not money, Mara. Success to me is helping people achieve their dreams."

"That's a beautiful sentiment, Joel." She looked at her hands. "I'm sorry, our past history is a big deal. I'm grateful for your help today. But it's one day compared to the fallout from the last time you had anything to do with my business. You're going to have to build my trust one day at a time. Can you understand that?"

"Fair enough. Let me share what I've learned since then as a start. Okay?" Joel turned in his seat and leaned back on the window.

Mara nodded.

"God had a plan for my life. It wasn't to keep getting richer and taking over companies. It's for me to help other people live out the purpose in their lives with the wisdom I've learned in mine and in business. I'm a happier person for it."

Mara's forehead drew together in small furrows above her nose. She sat silent for several minutes. Bridger Pack and Rescue would have been swallowed up into a huge catalog corporation and moved out of state. Joel had to know the importance of a sales pitch — to sell himself to someone whom he'd already burned. Sales 101: If he spoke first, he'd lose. And she knew it.

"I've made amends with everyone I hurt except you, Mara. Rich stopped me before I managed a hostile takeover."

"So you want me to believe you've changed and my former coach is behind this?"

"Yes." He didn't flinch. "Your family business succeeded because of your artistic and strategic talents. Rich helped me understand that, without you, the company would have become just another plant making substandard backpacks instead of the high-quality rescue gear that attracted me in the first place."

"Why would Rich send you, of all people, when he knew what you'd done? Why would he think I'd want anything to do with you?" Mara shook her head slightly trying to wrap her mind around the situation.

"Rich mentored me in business, but he also led me to Christ. I thought I knew what I wanted. I found out my dream was pretty empty. Rich felt our faith would make us more compatible than the other potential coaches." He chuckled, "Rich actually told me this would be a hard sell."

Mara's smile flittered across her lips as fast as the snow skittered across the hood. "How do I know for sure? How do I know I can trust you? I knew my account was reassigned, but I didn't know it would be you. I would never have —"

"Mara, I wanted the challenge because I owed it to you." Joel reached under his winter coat into his suit pocket. "I brought a personal letter of introduction. Normally you'd get an e-mail and a phone introduction first. But you needed someone right now for this leap in business size. Rich thought you'd give me a chance if I came in person with his recommendation. He believes in you, your company, and that I'm the best one to help you at this crossroad."

She tilted her head and squinted at him trying to gauge his real intentions.

He held a steady gaze as he handed her the envelope.

After the longest moment, Mara reached for the letter. She looked back over the seat to Cadence, who stayed ominously silent with her arms wrapped around her torso.

Mara slipped a peachy manicured nail under the flap, opened the letter, and read. She murmured a thoughtful "hmm" or "huh" interspersed with a side-glance in his direction now and then. She slipped page one behind page two.

"So you've doubled your business." She folded the letter and tapped it against her palm.

"Mara, I've done that several times. Most companies come to a hurdle like that and can't leap it. But I've done it and have successfully helped others in the two years since I've been coaching with Business Mentors."

She nodded, not to agree, but more to give herself time to take his measure. Mara considered Joel with her peripheral vision as she held the referral in front of her. The letter from Rich asked her to forgive and to trust Joel's guidance. Rich reminded her of the last-minute stop Joel had put on the takeover. She had choices and she turned them over in her mind. One would be to fire Business Mentors, Inc. But they'd been coaching her seven years, since a year into Bridger Pack and Rescue, when David found them through a referral. Education in marketing budgets and funding taxes to match company growth kept the company afloat with the surge forward. With her design work and David's fearless direction, the company grew too fast. They both needed guidance in upper-level financial management. Not something Mara had ever visualized herself doing.

Building the company had been David's idea. He wasn't the kind of man who worked well for someone else. He was a "type A" risk taker all the way. A passion matched to Mara's own intense personality, minus the risk-taking gene.

The acceptance of the contract activated the need for immediate hiring and training. Now she had to stay off her foot right when she most needed to do the hiring and train-ing frenzy. No wandering among the work-tables at the shop. It'd be hard enough to sit on the couch managing her least favorite chore, the finances. She'd somehow have to get the next batch of employees hired and trained on the new specialized cutting, sewing, and embroidery machines. Her newest designs for the U.S. Search and Rescue Exhibition team needed to be loaded in the system and materials ordered to fulfill military rescue team gear on deadline. No, there would not be time to track down a new company or find a coach who knew her business. Maybe Rich would take her back.

"When is Rich retiring?"

"Next month. He knew you were really close on this and went over everything in detail with me right down to your hiring applications and test results of the applicants."

"Did he now?" Great. The one person she didn't trust is the one person who knows everything about her and her business.

"Mara, I came because Rich handpicked me. He knew you needed me and not someone else. You need my experience to leap this next business wall. Please let me help you."

Cadence popped over the middle of the console. "Well, you sold me. Dude, you doubled your biz? That's like crazy! How much was it worth when you sold it? Did you make a lot of money?"

"Cadence!" Mara twisted in her seatbelt and smacked her ankle into the sidewall.

"Ow! Ow, ow, ow!" She bit back a scream. She tucked her head and breathed in, out, in. Sharp needles stung the back of her throat as she blinked away tears.

Joel touched her hand lightly. "Do you have the prescription?"

Mara nodded and kept her face averted. He would not see her cry. Not one wet drop. She'd already shown too much helplessness.

"Yes." She leaned back against the headrest.

"Cadence, give me directions to the pharmacy, okay?" Joel asked.

After getting the prescriptions filled, Mara took a painkiller immediately. They headed home, and Joel pulled into Mara's driveway. "Let me help you in and get your foot propped up."

Mara didn't balk. She had no more energy. The pain pill zapped her of any fight as it began to work. The snow had piled up several inches in a short time. Mara let Joel put his arm around her back instead of using both the new crutches. She wished she'd had the wheelchair from the hospital, but it couldn't have pushed through all the snow in her drive anyway. And neither could she. The hopping on one leg killed her with every jarring motion even with one crutch, the medicine, and Joel's support. It must have shown all over her face because up she went again into Joel's strong arms.

"I think you gained a little weight with your new fashion statement," he teased, with a nod toward her purple cast.

She glared back at him. "I didn't ask to be carried again." And she liked purple. If she had to wear an eyesore at least it'd be her favorite color. Besides, white would be a mess and black, though a better match for her business attire, seemed gothic.

Her son opened the front door. An exuberant Louie danced paw to paw, happy to see his people return as he drummed out a tempo on yet another door. The thump of his tail matched the throb in her leg.

"Dude. What happened, Mom?"

Was "dude" the only word her kids knew? The painkiller hit her brain. She felt more like she was on a merry-go-round than being held in a handsome man's arms. She grabbed for his strong shoulders and blinked hard. *Oh, boy.*

A delicious steamy scent of Mexican spices made her mouth water.

Cadence pushed Toby away from the door, "Back off. Mom broke her ankle and is on drugs."

"I'm not on drugs." She felt fuzzy and she knew it. Was it better to know you were losing it or to be clueless? Mara fought for a rational response. "It's a subscription."

Toby roared with laughter. "Subscription." Cadence joined in with a giggle though she tried to suppress it.

Clueless. Much better to be clueless.

"Toby, that's no way to treat your mama," Mrs. Calder chided as she came from the kitchen. He straightened up at her chastisement. "Now hop to and finish setting the table like I asked. Mr. Ryan, you'll be eating, I assume? I made a great big pot of cheater chili. A little of this, a little of that, and you have it. Now let's get our Mara comfy." She pointed at the recliner. "My, my, that sure is a doozy of a cast, isn't it? Dear, do you need some jammie pants? I can run get those." She scooted as fast as her wheeled walker would let her toward the back of the house.

Toby held it together just long enough for Mrs. Calder to clear the room, then burst into laughter. He fell backward onto the couch repeating *subscription* and *jammie pants.* The deadpan expression and held breath exploded from Cadence as she doubled over in laughter, too.

Mara's brain, while foggy and on drugs as her daughter claimed, didn't catch the joke. But Joel shook. He shook in little ripples from a rumble deep in his chest. He had the good grace to keep from bursting out in raucous laughter like her kids. However, that didn't help with the feeling that she'd turned into a bowl of jiggling JELL-O.

"Okay, put me, yeah, put me . . ." She couldn't finish. No one was listening and she couldn't remember the word she wanted to say anyway.

Cadence swatted her younger brother into a semblance of order. "I'm sorry, Mom, really. But you gotta know that was pretty funny."

Joel cleared his throat and tucked Mara into the recliner. She tugged on the lever. Her arms felt like spaghetti. Joel took over and helped her pull out the footrest.

"Hey what happened? I want in on the joke." Thirteen-year-old Marisa said, as she rounded the corner from the hallway. She stopped short at the sight of her mother. "D-u-d-e."

Yep, that was the only word they knew. Mara flopped against the brown leather in surrender.

"Oh, honey, it's no joking matter." Mrs. Calder shuffled up and put an arm around the young girl. "Your mama fell and broke her foot. Now come help me, all you kid-dos, come help carry dinner to the table.

Cheater chili to warm up the bones. Lots of healing garlic." She wheeled her way across the hardwood floors. "Come, come. Not you now, Mara dear. We're going to wait on you hand and foot. Oh, dear me, now I made a funny. Foot. Hand and foot." Her giggle echoed into the big kitchen.

"Maybe some of that, um, cheater chili would be a good thing for you." He had to get that recipe card for his mother's collection. The spicy aroma triggered sudden hunger signals. Joel's stomach rumbled.

He'd jumped on a plane out of LAX after an early breakfast, landed before lunch, and ended up at the hospital with his newest client for the rest of the day.

"It'll help combat the effects of that medicine if you have a full stomach." Joel started to follow the others into the kitchen. He stopped at the sound of a small snore. He turned back.

Mara's head tipped into the recliner's wingback. Understated elegance emanated from her even if the cast and tangled hair left her frayed around the edges. He watched for a second. Yes, there it was. Another small snore and a puff at the end finished it off. He resolved never to tell her. No-way-no-how would the proud and mighty Mara

Keegan take kindly to a fall from dignity. He grinned and went in for dinner. Well, maybe he'd never tell her. Or maybe they'd laugh about it. No, he'd probably never tell her.

4

Friday morning dawned through the arched living room window. Mara lifted a hand to block the bright sunshine. The fresh white snow magnified the rays off the window ledge. Someone had tucked a warm covering over her. She'd slept the entire night away safe in David's old chair.

Yesterday's events rushed back at her. Overwhelming. The only word she could think of to describe the mountain ahead of her. Now how would she get the quilt and her work done with the added limitations? With all the people to hire and train, an employee meeting announcing the new contract to plan, and updating all the government requirements, the quilt might get pushed to the bottom of her to-do list. Cadence's heart would be broken. She'd asked for this one thing for graduation.

Her cell warbled out Superman's theme. What? She didn't have that ring tone. It looked like her cell though, plugged into the charger right beside her. The caller ID said Superman and showed the logo too. This was crazy!

She picked up the phone. "Hello?" She cleared her throat and tried again, "Hello. Sorry. I need a drink of water."

"No problem, just ring the bell beside your chair." The voice had an amused tone.

"Joel?" Mara squinted over at the table again. Sure enough, her Liberty Bell souvenir from childhood stood ready with a note she read out loud, "Ring me for your every need."

"At your service."

"You're kidding, right?" Mara chuckled. "And who is going to answer that bell if you're on the phone and the kids are at school?"

"Give it a try."

With a bemused smile, Mara tinkled the four-inch copper replica.

A split-second later, Cadence dove out of the kitchen. She wore black pants, a white, button-up blouse, a black bow tie, and carried a folded white dish towel over her arm. "May I help you?"

"What in the world are you up to?"

"Hey, Mom," she smiled. "Got breakfast coming right up." Cadence ducked back in the kitchen for a moment and emerged with a silver tray laden with a china teacup setting and a crystal goblet of water. The goblet had a little gold charm of a piano around the stem. "But here's a coffee the way you like it to get you started. Your medicine is beside the lamp." Cadence served the steaming coffee with a flourish. She set the china cup and saucer on the side table within Mara's reach. It smelled divine.

"I don't know what to say except thank you."

"No biggie. We figured if you were stuck, then at least we'd make it fun for you." With a wink, "Hold it, rewind." She ran a hand over her face the way actors did. "It's my pleasure, madam." Cadence cut a short bow and then trotted off to the kitchen.

"What have you done to my children?" Mara said over the phone to Joel as she reached for the prescription. The throbbing seemed a little less. She'd try half the dose and see if she could keep a clear head. "Cadence even has her hair in a bun."

"Oh, nothing much." Joel's voice held a hint of a grin. "We had a business meeting over some great cheater chili last night. My mother is going to love that recipe, by the way. Two of your kids are at a school exhibition game today with plans to share duty tonight. Toby said school doesn't start until next Wednesday, but he'd signed up to help man the concessions. He took Marisa along to help out. So they're all set to take turns helping out at home too. Marisa has plans to make dinner with Mrs. Calder, who should be stopping over to take old Louie-boy for a walk shortly."

Mara set down the water glass after sipping it to swallow the pill. "Really. Quite the assumption you made setting up my family schedule." Mara wanted to be irritated. No irritation managed to bubble up. Especially when Cadence carried another tray of china out full of hot cinnamon rolls, strawberries and whipped cream, and a carafe to refill her coffee.

"Mrs. Calder agreed completely. The kids have your weekend all planned out. So sit back, relax, and get better. We need you down here as soon as you're able."

"Down here? Are you down at my office?" No one knew him. Did he saunter in and take over there too?

"Someone had to get the ball rolling. The contract's in play and we have new employees to get processed."

"How do you know what to do? And about the contract —"

"Mara, you have an excellent office manager in Jill Hilton. She's already pulled the interview files. You've made excellent notes and my company is sending the top applicant testing results over as we speak. And I just happen to be your business coach. I'd better know what I'm doing."

"But I —"

"Please trust me. There's nothing you can do today except start healing."

"I thought you would be on a plane today."

"I've extended for at least a week. If you need me, I can stay longer. My clients are coached mostly by phone with a few onsite visits as needed like this one. Those phone appointments are already set up on a schedule months in advance and I can call from anywhere in the country. Let me handle things down here until you can at least negotiate in and out of the house. I'll call you with any questions or if any emergency arises."

Mara tried to adjust to sit up higher in the chair, but her ankle sent throbbing pain up her leg. Joel was right. She squeezed her hand into a fist and pounded the chair arm. What if she didn't like the results? Cleaning up problems made by someone else could be devastating at this preliminary stage. She leaned on her sore shoulder and winced.

Then again, she wasn't in any shape to make decisions at the moment. But the only experience she'd had with Joel was in hostile takeover territory. Would the prescription painkillers interfere with her judgment? He had to be more rational than she could hope to be. "Okay. I don't seem to have any other option right now."

"No, you don't. But if you'll let your family take care of you and get better, I promise to keep you updated. A text for short important progress notes, an e-mail for longer ones, and a call if anything is urgent."

"Fine, fine." She was ready to hang up and then remembered the ring tone. "Hey, did you mess with my phone?"

"Your phone? No. I asked Cadence to find your charger and hook it up for you. Why?"

She felt the flush in her cheeks. Maybe she'd get out of it by a vague answer. "Nothing. My ring tone is different."

"Really? Nope, not me. What is it?"

Mara sighed, "Superman." She hung up on his chuckle. Not a chance would she tell him the Superman logo was the photo attached as well.

Mara waited long enough for the line to disconnect and dialed Jill's cell. "Hey."

"I wondered if I'd hear from you today," Jill responded. "There seems to be a very hot guy sitting at your desk and a rumor you are on a bit of a forced vacation. No, seriously, are you okay?"

Mara tried to adjust the blanket over her feet. "I'm so sorry. This was not in my plans." She couldn't toss the blanket end all the way over her toes. Toes so cold they almost matched the purple cast.

Jill laughed, "No, I suppose it wasn't. But you just get healed up. Joel and I have the office covered for you."

Mara's spirits lifted with Jill's upbeat demeanor. "I bet you were a bit surprised." A niggle of guilt lodged in Mara's gut. The workload already stretched Jill's regular hours. "Thank you for always being so flexible and reliable."

"Surprised for sure. But I'm more worried about you. How are you feeling? Joel says you're off your feet for two weeks. What in the world did you do?"

"Banged myself up by falling . . ." She cringed at the laughter she knew was coming. "Off my work stool."

Jill's infectious laughter lilted across the connection. "Only you."

"And I hate this loopy feeling, but it hurts to move around much yet." She stifled a groan that came out more like a lowing cow

64

as she tried to stretch a little. Both of them giggled.

"I'm sorry for laughing." She settled down. "I just can't believe it. Okay, I do have to say Joel told me about the colorful cast."

"Well, the choices were rather limited." Mara laughed with her again. "You should see it from where I'm sitting. I'm lucky I didn't wake up with faces drawn on my toes. You know my kids."

"Oh well, sounds like I'd better get over there and remind them. Or bring you some socks. Is there anything I can do?"

"Mrs. Calder and Joel have my kids all set up to wait on me. So nothing personally at the moment."

"Did I have any doubt?"

Mara could hear the humor in Jill's voice. She knew Jill had grown as fond of Mrs. Calder as of Mara's family. She'd eaten many a meal with them prepared by the beloved neighbor. "Jill, I do need something business-wise."

"Aren't you supposed to be recouping?"

"I know. But I have to ask you to be my lifeline."

"You know me. I'm not letting anything go by the wayside," Jill reassured Mara. "Joel seems smart and understanding.

Besides, he's got to know how to run this business since he's your coach and all. He is your coach, right? He told me he's Rich's replacement."

"Yes, he is. For now. But we don't have a history together like I did with Rich." Mara shot into the real reason for her call. "Listen, I need you to do something for me. I need you to keep me up on what's happening. And please don't mention it to Joel. I don't want him to feel like I'm Big Brother or something. I know he should know what he's doing but I would just feel safer. Okay?"

"I'm your eyes and ears here. This place matters as much to me as to you. I'll let you know if anything goes off track." Jill agreed. "You are my boss and my friend. You can count on me."

"I know that, Jill. You've been such a blessing over the years and especially since David died. Thank you for being someone I can count on."

Mara hung up and immediately felt helpless and lost. Every day for years, she'd risen by six and would be in her office by seven-thirty. Once the kids caught the school bus, she'd fly out the door. Now forced to sit still, her worldview suddenly altered in the ultra-quiet house.

She ate breakfast under the watchful eye

of the magpie in the tree outside the living room window. What else could she do?

When Mara finished eating, she called out. "Cadence?"

The affectation of a butler came from the kitchen, "Please ring the bell for service."

She played along and jingled. When Cadence responded, Mara asked for help to get ready for the day. She felt grungy after sleeping in her clothes. Her pajamas lay untouched and still folded on the coffee table within reach.

"Absolutely, madam, and then for your entertainment I have collected certain, shall we say, quilting items." Her eyes twinkled with presumption.

"Oh, you are a smart one." Mara's smile grew. "I might have a need for a little help to get the pictures done for your quilt squares. I didn't get them all printed onto the transfer paper before I fell. Then they need to be taken down to Tina and ironed onto the poplin blocks I've already cut out. You game?" Mara watched her daughter's face light up.

"Your wish is my command." Cadence pulled something from behind David's chair. "Mrs. Calder offered some assistance after the struggle you had with the crutches in the snow." She unfolded a walker with wheels. "But she suggested you keep Superman employed."

"Oh, no. No one is carrying me around any more." Mara shook her head. "Now you're turning me into an old lady, too?" But her lips tilted up. She knew it would be much easier to maneuver the walker and less painful on her arms, palms, and shoulders. Mrs. Calder's thoughtfulness knew no bounds. She was a true treasure. Without Miriam Calder, Mara had no clue how she'd have made it through the last three years. Since Mr. Calder passed away years ago, the octogenarian had become a second mother and grandmother to the Keegans.

Cadence helped her mother to balance her left knee on the walker's little fold-down platform seat. Then they inched their way down the long hall to the bathroom with Louie in close pursuit. He followed Mara everywhere. She was his person. Cadence left her for a moment of privacy and returned with a clean set of casual exercise clothes.

"See, with these stretchy pants you have plenty of room to get the cast through and they'll be comfy all day. Or if you prefer, you can wear your jammie pants." She couldn't get the line out without a snort.

"Uh-uh. I think I'll take the stretchies,

thanks." Mara wanted to reach out and smooth her fingertips over Cadence's cheek like she did when Cadence was a little girl. But to tempt this sweet truce wasn't worth the risk. They'd been barking at each other all year. Better to capture the moment in her heart than to scare away the sweetness. Oh, but she wished she could.

"So I had an idea for your hair. Instead of the shower, why don't we try the handheld in the tub with a lawn chair? I can wash your hair and then you can sit while I dry it."

Mara looked at her daughter again with a new respect. "Good thinking." There's the creativity of a brilliant mind. One more way Cadence took after her father. He had spectacular problem-solving skills.

A few moments later, Mara lay on a thick beach towel covering a chilly plastic chair brought in from the cold garage. Her daughter cradled her head with one hand and worked on her hair with the other. Cadence then spent quite a while French-braiding her hair into a beautiful plait ending at her waist. She actually felt pretty, too, with light makeup and clean clothes. Almost dolled up enough to go out, except for the crazy cast on her left leg and maybe the doctor's orders.

Exhausted from the hour's efforts of freshening up, Mara sat down in David's recliner again. The chocolate brown leather molded around her back as if David hugged her. Mara closed her eyes as a dreamy moment stole her away to his arms. He used to hug her when she'd plop into his lap. He'd run a hand into her hair and massage her scalp. Then he'd pull her close to lean against his warm shoulders. She leaned into the chair back. The leather felt cool against Mara's cheek. Not quite the same as a live husband. The arms that held her yesterday were not quite the same either. But she'd felt secure in them. Very secure. She missed the warmth of a man's embrace. Mara pulled the blanket off the back and snuggled into it for a short nap.

When she woke half an hour later, Mara at least felt halfway human and a little comforted as Cadence brought the box of photos out of the workroom. Mara pushed herself into an attentive position to see what could be salvaged. A mish-mashed out-of-order pile, bent up, and a little less pristine than before. None seemed too ruined for use on the quilt.

"My plan is to finish picking twenty-five photos. Then if you'll scan them and print each one on a T-shirt transfer, we can have the T-shirt shop use their big press to put them on the quilt blocks. Okay?" Mara dipped into the box. She picked up the top picture and admired the frilly look Cadence used to love. *Used to* being the prime descriptive. Princess this. Princess that. Everything was princess. Mara watched Cadence for a hint of that little girl again. No more dresses for her, not since junior high. Ruffles, ribbons, and rainbows all gone. Lace replaced by jeans and tanks and hoodies.

"Why not just iron them here?"

"Household irons can't get enough heat and pressure to seal the transfer to the material. It wouldn't last as long. I tried that on the small quillow I made with all your grandparents' photos on it. I learned my lesson when they washed off too fast."

"Well, sure, I can print them for you."

Crinolines and tiaras all wrapped up in her father's embrace. The best possible daddy memory. She could embroider Daddy's Little Princess on the block. "Be sure to use the photo setting on the copier."

"I know, Mom, I'm the one who taught you. Remember?" Cadence sat down on the arm of the chair as she waited for the first few. "So do I get to pick out any pictures?"

Mara glanced up. She'd planned to choose

them herself as part of the gift. "I hadn't thought of that, honey. I wanted to do all of it. You're not supposed to make your own gift." Would she leave out important memories?

"Mom, I want to do more than that. I want to learn how to make a quilt."

"I know, but this one is supposed to be made for you not by you. You could help me with the next one though."

"When?" The world turned on edge with the sharpness in her voice. "I'm going to college. When am I going to learn? And isn't this quilt supposed to be about my memories of my life? Isn't it about passing on the tradition? When have you had time to do any of that?"

Mara couldn't quite tell with the effects of the medicine if her voice remained calm. She worked extra hard to modulate the tones. "I have some surprises planned. I'd really rather keep them as surprises." Bzzt. Wrong answer. She watched Cadence's face lose the final vestiges of friendliness. Not once in three years did it seem as a mother she could make the right decisions. Her daughter pulled further and further away emotionally.

This last day felt like a miracle truce and she'd spoiled it by locking out the daughter she tried to draw in. She had to compromise even if it meant blowing a surprise. "What if you help me pick the photos and we sketch out a design together today? I had an idea, but you're right." Mara covered Cadence's knee with her hand. "This quilt is about you. Maybe you won't like what I have in mind."

"Really? I'd love that!" Cadence threw her arms around Mara.

"Ow, ow, ow, honey." Okay, compromise had its merits even when painful. "My shoulder's still bruised."

"Oops, sorry. I didn't think a hug would hurt you."

"Your hugs are always wonderful. I'll be okay." The first hug in months and the squashed shoulder sabotaged it. "What if you helped me over to the couch and we took some time to go through this box? There must be hundreds of pictures here."

Superman's theme, the short version, announced the arrival of a text message. "Who messed with my ring tones?" Mara touched the screen of her iPhone and slid her finger across the bottom of the screen to open the message.

"Don't you love it? Joel totally owns that one." Cadence beamed. "Marisa and Toby agree. Any guy who can carry you from the house to the hospital to the house again while single-handedly saving your business is Superman."

"He didn't single-handedly save my business. He just saved a contract."

"Yeah, right. That's nothing important or anything. Just some little project you've only been talking about for the last three years." Cadence whistled and then made the sound of a bomb explosion. "That's what would have happened."

"Nothing was going to explode, Cadence." Mara read the text message. Cadence peeked over at it.

"Contacting first-round applicants for sewing, embroidery machines, and have a great front runner for repair tech position."

"He's working fast. See? Faster than a speeding bullet — Superman." She had the gall to sing the name.

There was that I-told-you-so face that mimicked David's. "Yeah, we'll see. I need to be there." Mara texted Joel back a request for the applicant list. "I'll have him send it by e-mail so I can go over it."

A minute later the e-mail popped through to her inbox with an entire list of names and online links to their test results in teamwork, creativity, machine skills, and personality assessments.

"Wow, he is good," Mara mumbled, more to herself. He had to already have written the e-mail to get all the content into the body that fast.

"Now do you believe me? I'm a great judge of character."

The I-told-you-so smirk twice in a short time caused a twinge in Mara's heart. Her expression was too much like David's. The tinge of red in Cadence's hair, the tilt of her eyes, and certain mannerisms like that smirk brought warmth now instead of intense pain with the memories. A warmth that matured from the sharp stab of a new widow, to a mellow appreciation, each time she noticed something from her husband in one of her children.

Mara's eyes drank in David's essence as his expressions floated across her daughter's face. She'd thank God for the vision, if she were on speaking terms with him.

Mrs. Calder popped her head in the front door and rattled off a chain of thoughts. "Would Louie like a walk before lunch?" Louie scrambled to move off his second favorite dog bed and over to the front door. "The sun melted off the sidewalk snow the boys missed and I think we could go to the mailbox and back. How are you doing, dear?" She reached down to wiggle one of

Louie's fuzzy, floppy ears. He stretched out his neck as he closed contented eyes and moaned the moan of a happy dog.

"A little better today, thank you. And thank you so much for feeding my family last night."

"Well, it sure feels good to help out. Your family has been good to me over the years. I saved the leftovers so you could have a yummy lunch. You slept through dinner, dear. Right through. But that superman of yours said to just let you sleep. So I did. But not without saving you something for lunch today."

You, too, Mrs. Calder? It appeared Joel would be etched into a hall of fame soon if this crew could manage it. "That is so nice. Would you like to share a bowl with us?"

"Let me take this fellow out for you. I need to check if my mail has come yet. Waitin' for a letter from my sister. We're talking about taking a cruise. A cruise! Can you imagine? I could be floating on the ocean. Never did anything like that before. Robert was a bit more practical." She patted her thigh and the dog danced. "Mail it is, boy."

"I'll go nuke the chili. Then I can print out the pictures we have so far while you rest."

"I don't need to nap like a —"

"Mom, don't make me call Superman." She waggled her forefinger. "The doc said to rest."

Mara startled. She wouldn't. Cadence wouldn't dare call Joel to tattle on her. The crossed arms and stare-down told her otherwise. "Okay, you win. I'll rest while you get those printed. Then I'll show you what I've drawn out so far on the quilt design and you can make any changes you want. Are we good?"

"We're good." Cadence launched herself off the leather couch. "Chili coming right up."

5

Joel sat behind Mara's oversized table desk with a stack of applicant files. The lavender and light green plaid chairs, darker plum planter, and rich verdant plants exuded peace, though too feminine for Joel. Mara's presence and personality filled the room with the same understated elegance as if she were with him. He took hiring these people more seriously than he'd ever done in his own business. Mara would have to live with the decisions he made and as her coach, so would he.

She needed him. No, he corrected, the business needed him here until the key player could manage. It sure felt good to be needed though. He hadn't been needed in a long time.

This on-site visit proved to be a challenge with high stakes. Stakes beyond the normal challenge when one injured woman managed to invade his every thought. Add three teens, a guard dog, a Neighborhood Watch grandma, and a blizzard — the challenge rose to Olympic level. He grinned at the thrum of blood through his veins.

Joel called through the open door. "Jill?"

"Yes," she said as she stepped in and waited beside the matching cherrywood filing cabinets lining the far wall.

Jeans, everyone in Montana seemed to wear jeans everywhere. Jill looked professional from the top up. He'd have to help Mara polish the daily attire around here. "Can you go ahead and print the last batch of applicant tests? I don't want to tie up the printer in here."

"Sure, give me a few minutes."

"If you can do that, I'm about done with these and need to finish a few other things before we break for the night. I'll contact the new hires this weekend and Monday."

"You're going to contact folks over the weekend?"

"Training needs to start as early in the next week as possible. Let's shoot for an orientation this coming Tuesday afternoon. That leaves us Wednesday for any follow-up or to fill positions that don't work out for whatever reason."

Joel typed the tentative schedule into his calendar.

"Um, can I ask you something?"

He looked up. "Absolutely. Ask anything. Transparency is the first, most important business marker. Remember that, Jill, transparency fosters trust."

She thought for a moment then nodded. "Is Mara in good enough shape to look over your choices?"

"Yes. Yes, she is." He held out a yellow legal pad. "I've already put together not only my top choices, but also second runner-up options. I need that last group of tests to finalize it. Then would you type out this plan and send it to me as an attachment with the current team leader names and contact information?"

"Oh, sure, and thanks." Jill's worry lines relaxed. "I know Mara will really appreciate being kept apprised. I give her daily reports when she's on the road at buyer's shows or conferences."

Jill's help all day was already a huge benefit. She had organized everything so well all he had to do was ask and she provided exactly what he needed. Now she seemed to warm up to him without hesitation.

"I know this is a rough one, Mara's ankle and all the changes happening so fast. I want you to know that I plan to take these files by Mara's house when we close up shop for the night. Part of my job as her coach is to make sure she understands why I make certain suggestions. Normally she'd make these decisions after a session with me."

"Ah, well, that makes me feel a lot better. She's been good to me, you know." Jill walked to the door. "She's been worried about getting a new coach. I've been in on the phone sessions with Rich since Mara's husband died. I take notes so she can concentrate."

Joel nodded. "I can tell you're a huge blessing to Mara."

Jill blushed at his compliment. Her light coloring and natural blonde hair gave her no reprieve from the full flushed facial.

"Rich's an excellent coach. He's left me some big shoes to fill, that's for sure."

She smiled back, "Well, from the work you've put in today I can see you know your stuff. I'll do my best to keep up with you."

"What's he doing now?"

Jill answered, "He's fine, really, Mara. It's pretty quiet and going well right now."

"You're kidding. No problems?"

"I mean it. In the hour since we last talked, no problems." Jill giggled. "Other than he looks out of place in very feminine office décor. He seems to live what he preaches. He actually told me that transparency fosters trust."

Jill would tell her if she should be concerned. They'd become a solid team since it'd gone to a one-owner shop. "Is there anything I should know?"

"The guy looks good surrounded by lavender?" Her voice teased over the line. "Pastels suit him. But I bet he looks great in blue."

Mara stared at the ceiling. *And now Jill falls to Superman's heroism.* She sighed. *Was there anyone left that hadn't succumbed besides herself?*

"Joel will be by tonight to go over his top picks for the new positions."

"Good. I don't think I can handle all this without knowing what's going on." She rubbed her eyes. "All this out-of-touch stuff is driving me nuts!"

"Yep, I can tell. But you sound tired. Are you really up for work right now?"

"Of course I am. I'm a klutz, not incapacitated." *Almost.* She shrugged. The movement caused an involuntary gasp of pain as she dropped the phone into the fold of a blanket on her lap. Mara closed her eyes at the spasm and retrieved the phone. "Sorry, dropped my cell." She cradled her left shoulder as she kept her tone light. She didn't want to deceive Jill, but it had to be done. Her number-one employee needed to be the first person to believe in her abilities. "We have a contract to fulfill and people to employ."

"You are one focused woman. Would this be a high-five team moment if you were here?" Jill punctuated her contagious enthusiasm by a slap on the desk as she imitated the sound of a high-five.

Glad Jill hadn't picked up on her weakness, she said, "Oh, yes, right back at you!" Mara looked around her. No wood close enough to smack without causing significant pain. "You'll just have to take my word that I'm high-fiving you in spirit."

"Works for me," Jill said.

Mara's voice took on the edge of a private detective. "So, what can you tell me so far about this guy? What's he like to work with?"

"Joel is hunkered down and in the hunt for excellent employees. He's serious, careful, and I think you'll be pleased. And between you and me, if I weren't married, I'd sure be asking him out for a coffee right about now. Hoo yah, what a cutie!"

"Okay already, I totally admit he is attractive." Mara couldn't get his blue eyes out of her head any more than she could get Montana out of her soul. It was probably the pain medicine. It made her loopy. "But you are on the lookout for any nonsense, right?"

"Right. But only if you'll stay home and get some rest and r-e-l-a-x. We've got this handled. Don't get me wrong, we want you back fast. But just let someone else shine for a change, would you?"

"Fine, fine." Had they all conspired to force recuperation on her? "Where am I going to go with my whole left side out of commission anyway?" Then she looked at the length of the hallway and back at her purple appendage. Not even a simple traipse down to her home office. She had to accept help, but she'd make this sense of dependence as short as possible.

"Hah, it figures. That's the only way I'll be able to pin you down. What about the kids?"

"That's the interesting part. My kids are taking turns taking care of me. Mrs. Calder came over and fixed dinner. I hear she's planning to do that all week. Cadence showed me a written schedule complete with a meal plan." Mom pride won as she bragged, "You wouldn't believe the organization and responsibility my kids are taking on for me."

Jill whistled into the phone. "Now I'll say you have some kind of luck, cast or no cast."

"No, just good people in my life like you and Mrs. Calder. Always give credit where credit's due."

"Uh-huh." Jill sounded pleased at the compliment even as she reminded Mara, "Don't forget the new man in your life, Coach Joel."

"We'll have to see how that turns out."

"Oh, I almost forgot. Some executive assistant you have here." She joked as Mara heard the computer clicking on Jill's end. "Here's the daily reports for you."

Mara pinned the phone between her bad shoulder and her ear with a small wince. She opened her Mac with her good hand and checked the inbox. "Ah, now I'm feeling better." She scrolled down the daily financial report. "Thanks." But if she was feeling better, why did she have such a gloomy feeling in the pit of her stomach? It seemed that Joel had the office running quite well without her. Was he edging her out or protecting her interests?

6

"What do you mean you don't want this picture?" Mara transported back to the moment fixed on film. Cadence's great big grin showed red, white, and blue rubber bands crossing every which way on her silver braces. "Don't you remember that day?"

"Yeah, all too well. I remember feeling miserable and ugly. I mean U-G-L-Y, ugly." Her mouth formed the letters with dramatic flair. She tossed a long brown strand of hair behind her shoulder.

Mara watched her daughter's feigned indifference. Did she really have bad memories of her childhood like that? Was her entire childhood memory skewed from losing her father? She gentled her voice. "Do you know what I remember? Giggles and goofing and galloping gaggles of girls, that's what I remember." She kept the sentiment close to her heart. Cadence certainly couldn't see it through her mother's vision.

Cadence shrugged her shoulders.

Mara would give her the good parts. The kid-friendly highlights might help Cadence reassess those memories with a more mature perspective.

"I remember getting several bags of different-colored rubber bands on the way home from the orthodontist. Then your daddy brought twelve different tubs of ice cream, a bunch of toppings, and all the sprinkles he could find."

Mara remembered David's genuine pleasure when Cadence vaulted into his arms. He'd locked eyes with her as he hugged Cadence. Their private time later that night had been full of laughter over the long afternoon of ice cream and yard games. The memory of the kisses that followed pierced her heart. She pushed his kisses back into the past. Today was about her daughter, not her own loneliness.

"Oh, yeah! Then we made the biggest ice cream sundae in the world and tried to get *Guinness Book of World Records* to publish it." They both giggled. "My teeth hurt so bad and I couldn't chew anything for days. But having all that ice cream was cool."

"Eh, what's a little week of ice cream? I still can't believe we didn't win the biggest sundae though. That was huge! We had to invite over the whole neighborhood to eat it before it melted."

"People still call our house the ice cream house." Cadence's wistful gaze swung from the photo to Mara. "Didn't we get a picture of that? We should use that one."

"We could, but *Guinness Book of World Records* never returned it. Sorry, digital cameras still weren't as common as getting printed pictures made. That's one thing I do regret not listening to your dad on." Mara ran her hand across the photo of Cadence and cleaned off some dust from its visit to the workroom floor. A faint paw print complete with nail marks showed on the back of it. "Sometimes I think the reason a picture has a thousand words is the story behind the picture, not the image you can see. Don't you?" She thought of many pictures she could have had if she'd only listened to David.

"I guess so," Cadence admitted. "I still don't want it. I look so ugly."

Mara reached up to tuck the errant strand back behind Cadence's ear. She lightly cupped her daughter's cheek and hoped Cadence wouldn't disconnect as she had for the last few years. "Not only are you a beautiful young girl, but I love what happened after the ice cream party." Mara expected instantaneous recognition, but Cadence gave her a blank stare as she pulled away. "So many kids saw your Independence Day decorations that they did it too. Then when school started, all the girls who had braces started following your trend and wore bands to match their outfits."

"Oh, I remember! Every kid who had braces even wore school colors on game days," she laughed, "and the ones who didn't have braces started putting colored bands in their hair or finding spots to decorate shoes and clothes. It lasted all year!"

"You really are a natural leader. People follow your ideas." Mara hoped she'd conveyed a deep truth to Cadence. "And I picked up every color of the rainbow off the floor, in the sofa, and all over the house for a year! Your dad had to buy me a new vacuum after I sucked up one too many."

"Yeah?" Cadence took the picture from her mom. "Maybe this one does deserve a spot on the quilt. After all, this one day changed a year of my life."

Mara thought about Cadence's beautiful smile. "Mm, maybe a little more." She took Cadence's chin and tugged her face toward her. With a quick little peck on her daughter's cheek she said, "Show me that toothy grin, GirlieQ."

Cadence rewarded her with her perfectly straight pearly whites and an even more precious gift of not rubbing away her kiss.

"It's kind of taking longer than I thought. How 'bout I print the first dozen and get those iron-ons down to the T-shirt shop? Then you can rest a bit and work on the embroidery part while I do whatever else you need." She stood and headed toward Mara's workroom with a handful of pictures.

Had she pushed too far with the kiss? She missed the toddler with chubby cheeks who begged for mommy kisses and stories and the old rocking chair.

"We can work on more after we eat. I have a special cake recipe for tonight. Besides Superman's going to be hungry." She tossed the last line over her shoulder with an impish wink.

There's that little sprite. Mara's heart warmed. She called after Cadence, "Superman doesn't have to come to dinner every night, you know." She fought off another yawn. "We can finish picking out photos tomorrow."

At least she wasn't as loopy as last night. Her body's need for healing made her drowsy. She'd catnap while Cadence went out and forget the throbbing in her ankle. The other kids would be home soon if she needed anything. But tonight might not be the best one for Superman to come to dinner again. Tonight might make him uncomfortable.

Superman's theme filled the living room. She had to change that ring tone somehow. But one of the kids always switched it as a joke anyway. One minute she'd have a regular ring, set it down, and the next time she picked it up some wild new song exploded into the air. Her luck it might be the theme from *Rocky* or the *Transformers*. Might as well leave it alone. Besides, Joel would never hear it. It only happened when he called and he probably thought she'd already switched it.

"Hello."

Louie cocked his head though he never lifted it off his paws.

"Mara, Joel here."

"I know."

"The ring tone?"

She thought fast. "Caller ID. What's happening?" Mara sat up on alert. Louie sat up with her and wagged his tail. "Is everything okay?"

"Yes, no problems here. I wanted to check

in with you in person. I have a stack of files to go over with you tonight. Is it all right if I come by when the shop closes?"

"Of course, Jill said you would." Shoot, did that tip her hand that she was keeping tabs on him? "But go ahead and come on in when you get here, so I don't have to get up."

"Wouldn't dream of making you answer the door. I'll be there a little after six, if all goes as planned. Do you need anything? Can I pick something up for you?"

Where was this guy from? He sure didn't act like men she'd met lately. One major reason dating held no appeal. "No, but thank you." Maybe she should drop a hint. "Tonight's dinner, well, it's sort of a family thing."

"Maybe tonight is not a good night for work," Joel suggested.

"No, we need to talk. Come on over."

Tired of being ignored, Louie trotted over and bumped her hand for a petting. Mara slid her fingers under his neck and scratched around his blue collar. The dog sat at her side and tucked his muzzle on the sofa cushion.

"Do you need anything for dinner? I know Marisa's cooking with Mrs. Calder, but do they need anything?"

Wow, he really might be Superman. "No, I think the kitchen's handled. I've sent Cadence to pick up a few things for the quilt. If I can't work, at least I can be productive."

"You're working on the quilt? You should be resting."

Mara's defense mechanism jumped up like a killdeer racing away from her ground nest. "I was. You woke me up."

"No offense intended." He answered with a sincere voice. "I'm sorry."

"You don't understand. It's me. Just me." Her hands emphasized the words though no one sat across from her but the dog. "I've got very little time available as it is, and now this. I have to spend the time wisely. If I can't work at least I can get this chore done and out of the way."

Cadence came in the front door and stopped at Mara's words. The happy face disappeared into a bland expression as Mara's older relatives had done. They chose not to show emotion or telltale tics when dealing with someone not from the reservation. Cadence ignored Louie's greeting as her eyes dulled behind a screen of you-don't-love-me. She had held a grudge against her mother through high school, since Mara had missed one too many special performances.

"Hang on, Joel," Mara said quickly. "Honey —"

Cadence tossed the bag she held over to the couch. "Here." She hung up her coat and scarf on the wooden coat tree. Louie danced at her feet. His toenails clicked a scratchy rat-a-tat on the wood floor. "Stop it! Go lie down."

Joel asked, "Was that Cadence?"

Louie slinked back to his dog pillow and lay down without circling. His nose poked tightly between his paws as he watched Cadence intently.

"Joel, I have to go. I'll see you at six." Breathe deep. Her daughter just misunderstood. Mara never felt more trapped than now with her purple appendage. She might as well be calf-roped. "Cadence? Please come back here."

Mara leaned to see around the archway dividing the living room and dining area. Why couldn't Cadence see how hard she tried to be everything to everyone? How many people and directions pulled at her since David died? She didn't want to be a widowed working mother.

"No, thanks, I have *chores* to do." She emphasized the offensive word as she disappeared into the sunny kitchen and took a dark storm cloud with her.

There it was. The same word thrown back at her as an accusation. "Honey, I can't chase you down. Please?"

A begrudged monotone responded. "Can't. Gotta get stuff done."

Mara plopped her elbow on the couch arm and nestled her forehead against her palm. So much for the progress of the afternoon. Tonight of all nights. Could God punish her any more? How was she supposed to be father, mother, breadwinner, boss, artist, and whatever other overwhelming job on her to-do list that teetered every day like a stack of china? Since David died, she'd lost touch with her children. She hadn't even had a decent mourning period because she had so many legalities to work through with the business, estate, and finances. After the funeral, Mara lost track of the appointments with lawyers to draw up new paperwork for the business and handle the insurance policies. That was the beginning of the lost family time. And she had a sudden craving for a giant ice cream sundae.

Joel tapped on the front door. As he peeked inside, Louie stood, but Mara's flat palm signal held the dog in place on the big cushy bed. Joel watched Mara flick her palm down and point a finger at the floor.

"He's really well trained." Joel looked from Mara to the dog and back to Mara.

"You can come in." She closed the drawing pad on her lap and laid a colored pencil on it.

He stepped inside, arms full of files. "Did you say something to Louie before I opened the door?"

"Nope. He's sign language trained."

"Sign language? Like real sign language?"

"No, just hand signals we made up." She tried twisting to put the art supplies on the end table, but winced at the stretch. "Can you?" Mara held the notebook out toward Joel.

Joel crossed the large living room to set down his stack and take the materials. He found a spot for her pile and then dropped a large, overstuffed computer bag on the floor. He nudged his chin toward Louie. "So he's a pretty smart pooch."

"Oh, I'll say. Took me a couple months to realize he was trained to signals. Not for him though, but because I realized I'd been doing the hand motions when I gave the command without thinking about it. One day I had a mouthful of cookie, and I wanted him to stay when the kids ran in the

96

door. I threw out my hand and couldn't get the words out because the cookie was so dry." A smile lit up Mara's face. Her brown eyes caught the glow from the overhead ceiling light. Joel caught his breath at the soft beauty touched with a hint of exotic. "The dog stopped dead still and so did the kids. It surprised all of us. So I tried another one. I pointed down like you just saw me do. And the old boy did it. Well, he wasn't so old then." Her face took on a misty appearance.

He hadn't taken his eyes off Mara. A beautiful quilt full of Native American designs in purples, turquoise blues, and yellows wrapped around her legs. The colors enhanced the lavender jogging suit jacket she wore and deepened the effect of her mahogany hair and eyes. "Wow. That's something." Joel was sure he meant the dog story. Didn't he? Yes, the dog was quite something. He swallowed another "Wow."

She looked back up at him. "Too bad the kids didn't keep following the hand signals." She grinned. "After that we kept trying all sorts of commands. If they were new ones, he'd learn them in a few days. Balancing a treat on his nose and catching it, that one he learned in three tries."

Joel laughed. "How many can he do?" He

still hadn't looked at this miracle of a dog. She kept his attention.

"I've never really counted. Hmm. All the normal dog tricks and commands." Mara ticked off her fingers. "Plus a few just for fun. But truthfully, when he closes a door for me I think that's pretty gentlemanly of him." She held a straight face.

"Huh?" Joel hadn't been ignoring her. But he did get a little lost in watching her. "Sorry, did you say he can close doors?"

"Of course. Want to see?" She pointed at the front door.

"Oh! I, uh, got caught up in the conversation." *Not staring at you.* He made a move to stand and correct his mistake when Mara laid her hand on his arm.

"Let him show off." She snapped twice to get the dog's attention. Louie's head popped up. Mara pointed at the open door. Then held her open hands side by side in front of her. She brought her thumbs together mimicking an open door. Then closed them by hinging them into a closed prayer position. Louie shot across the glossy wood floor, leapt up to the doorknob, and walked on his hind feet to shut the door.

"I'm impressed."

Louie dropped back down on all fours and stood waiting for Mara's next command.

She flicked the fingertips of one hand. He darted over to her for a session of praise and snuggles. "I got tired of the kids leaving the door wide open all seasons. So for a few days I played with him secretly. Then I showed the kids. After that, I never had another open door again. It was too much fun for them all."

"That is some dog! Remind me to watch for your sign language. I wouldn't want to get attacked and not see it coming."

"Well, that's our other little secret." She rubbed fuzzy ears. "He's never, ever been trained to attack. He just barks and growls."

"So you mean in the office yesterday, he'd have never come after me?"

"No, probably not. He'd have licked you to death first."

"Why, that tricky Mrs. Calder. Neither of you told me and she certainly didn't." Joel hunkered down beside the sleek, black dog and held out his hand. He received a warm lick and then a nudge for some petting. "Look at that, boy, you're in cahoots with this lady."

Mara tossed her head back and giggled. "I told you it was a secret. Since David died, it feels a little safer to let people think Louie's a guard dog."

Smart woman. Correct that. Beautiful,

smart woman who owns a smart dog. Joel admired her creative mind. Sure, yeah, that was it. He'd never met a woman quite like this one. No wonder she'd built a small company into one he'd tried to take over. He straightened up as the cold washed over his soul. He had a lot of amends to make with her to earn her trust.

Marisa ran through the living room and waved. "Hey, Superman." She hadn't called him anything but Superman since last night when they'd excitedly praised him over dinner for carrying Mara over the snow. Helping her with algebra before he headed to his hotel cemented her admiration.

He waved at the young girl.

"Dinner will be ready as soon as Mrs. Calder finishes teaching me to make stroganoff with mushrooms and gravy. It was one of my dad's favorites. I'm helping while Cadence makes dessert."

"Hey, how'd the math test go?" He called at her disappearing back.

She grabbed the kitchen doorjamb and swung back in, "I so aced it!"

He laughed as they gave each other a thumbs up. "Good job, Marisa."

Joel sat down on the couch beside Mara who appeared a bit bemused by the banter. Her wide eyes soaked in the comfort and trust between her youngest and Joel. "Let's take a look at the contract, shall we?" Joel mentally tucked away the fact he may have gained a point in Mara's esteem. The sun may have sunk outside, but the hope in his chest beamed bright.

7

Mara squirmed in discomfort. She'd been sitting all day, plus the hour since Joel arrived establishing their nightly schedule. She needed to stretch, but was still a tad afraid to cause herself more pain.

"Are you okay?" Joel asked.

Mara rolled her lips in together and tried to lift her cast off the pillow. "I just need to make it down the hall for a minute." She looked across the great room and into the dark hallway. The spaciousness of the home, always her favorite feature, now loomed as villainous territory for the simple trek to the bathroom.

"Here let me help you."

She wanted to crawl under the house. This was her business coach not her preschool teacher. On top of that he was quite a handsome man. Having him help her to the bathroom was like the nightmare birthing story Jill told of the gorgeous doctor that showed up to fill in for her vacationing physician. Oh, no way. She'd call Cadence or one of the other kids first.

Joel pushed off the couch and looked around. "Where's the crutches?" Louie saw the movement and unwound from his pillow.

"I'm not using them. Mrs. Calder loaned me one of her walkers."

He suppressed a grin. "Really?"

"Fine, fine." She waved a hand. Louie trotted across the room and ducked his head. He sniffed around the floor then looked back at her for more direction. "Poor Louie, I'm not talking to you boy." Mara rubbed his furry cheek. "It's behind the arm of the sofa here."

Joel pulled it out. He unfolded the contraption and then gave it to Mara. "Hang on a minute. I can push the coffee table out of the way for you so you can go straight."

"Thanks, that's really nice." Joel's thoughtfulness seemed to have no end. Did he always think one step ahead?

"I'll be here to be sure you don't fall."

"Now I do feel like an old lady," she joked. A warmth spread through her heart as the distance across the huge home didn't appear quite as daunting as a few moments ago. Joel's protective chivalry comforted her somehow. She'd missed that part of having a man around. A lot. She missed an arm around her in church. She missed date night. She even missed the drudgery of yard work while David would tell her all his ideas.

Joel helped Mara lift off the couch and settle on the walker frame. Then she didn't move. "I'm feeling a bit awkward here."

Joel produced the bell. "Maybe this will help." His features softened into compassion. Those cute crinkles fanned out turning his eyes into his star feature. Man, he was handsome!

Mara would never take walking a few feet for granted again. The marvel of the human body amazed her. She rang the bell and Marisa ran to help.

"Hey, Mama, what's the scoop?" Her coloring matched her mother's more than her dad's. Less reddish hue in her hair and more golden skin than Cadence's. As a baby, friends and family called her Mini-Mara. She still had her mother's look. Mara lifted Marisa's hair off her shoulder and smoothed it behind her ear, grateful this daughter didn't mind a little affection. Cadence hadn't come close since the earlier misunderstanding.

"Want to help me that way?" She dipped her head in the general direction of the bathroom.

"You betcha. I've been hoping to get a turn to take care of you. Bringing a glass of water doesn't really count. You kinda don't need me that much." Louie paced himself beside Mara's walker the same as he did for Mrs. Calder's round-the-block exercises.

"Oh, GirlieQ, of course I need you." The dog pressed between the wall and the walker frame. Louie yelped all of a sudden and sprawled on the floor with a thud.

Mara startled. "Did I get you with this thing?" Louie wagged his tail, thumping it on the wood floor. With as much pounding as the floor and furniture took, Mara was amazed it all didn't fall apart. Louie needed a minute and a little help from Marisa to stand up. "I didn't feel you. Did I roll over a paw?" She reached out and scratched his ears. "Good boy. So sorry."

"Everything all right?" Joel called from the sofa.

"Yes. I think I smushed a doggie paw or something. Marisa's checking it." She watched Louie, but he didn't limp or show any further discomfort. "He seems okay."

On her return, she noticed Joel intent on the pages in her sketchpad. He looked mesmerized.

"Okay, boy, go lie down." She flicked the

signal. Louie trotted over to his dog bed, circled several times, and curled up to sleep.

"I hope you don't mind, Mara. This is beautiful." He turned the page to show her what he admired. "Is it the quilt design?"

"Yes. You like it?" A ripple of pleasure skated over her.

"It looks like a reversed stained glass window. So creative."

Joel set the sketchbook down. He stood to make Mara comfortable. Marisa stored the walker back beside the couch arm and Joel pulled the coffee table up. Then he grabbed the flat pillow and helped Mara prop her leg up in front of her on the coffee table.

Mara sighed, "That's perfect." She glanced at the wall clock. She could take her meds a few minutes early and maybe think of a few other needy-like things so Marisa felt more involved caring for her. "Marisa, I think I'm ready for another dose of medicine and something to drink, but water's a little bland right now. Do we have anything else?"

"Coming right up." Marisa took off to the kitchen. She returned with a glass of sweetened raspberry tea for her mother.

"Thanks, GirlieQ." She tipped the glass in a salute. "Just what I needed. You know, normally I feed Louie before dinner. Could you do that for me?"

"Hey, Fuzzy-Face, chow time." Marisa ran back into the aroma of a cake baking with the dog at her heels. The sweet cake scent mingled with sounds of a mixer and Cadence's voice asking for more butter.

Joel already had the page open again. "How are you going to get the look of stained glass like this on a quilt?"

"If Cadence likes it, we'll get rich colored fabrics and I'll create a scale model of each of the pieces to match the designs. Then we cut out pattern pieces and cut the fabric to match the patterns. The finishing effect will be finding the right material to act like the soldering between glass pieces."

"It's going to be a lot of intricate work, isn't it?"

"Yes, but worth every minute when the art I'm creating is for someone special I love. I especially enjoy designing and then seeing it come to life." There's that star feature again. His eyes could be the center on a star quilt radiating out vibrant life. She stared, unable to break the electricity between them until he spoke. "I just want Cadence to know she's loved. Quilts make you feel loved, you know?"

"What goes in the blank spots?" He traced a finger around the drawing. "It's like the stained glass is the frame and there's empty windows. And they're even arched cathedral style."

"Those windows are for the photo transfers." She gestured toward the floor. "Can you grab that bag at your feet?"

Joel handed it to Mara.

She reached in and pulled out an off-white rectangle. "See? This part isn't ready to sew yet into the quilt top. I have little captions to embroider under the photo like this one." Mara held up the Powwow Princess block she'd finished embroidering that afternoon. It showed Cadence as a young girl in a native dance move. She wore a traditional Crow outfit of a soft hide dress, moccasin boots, and a beautiful belt. Colorful beading covered the leggings of the boots and matching belt.

He looked fascinated. "Did you do her costume too?"

She gently educated Joel. "We don't call it a costume. That's a little insulting. Each of the pieces of her outfit took months of handwork. My mother and grandmother designed it for her."

"That's incredible!"

Mara sent a secretive peek around the area. "I have another surprise I can't wait to do for Cadence. I'm going to add some

108

beadwork like my grandmother taught me. Cadence liked it when she was a little girl. But then she lost interest."

"Beads on the quilt — like how? How does all that fit together?"

Mara took the sketchbook from Joel, flipped to a page a few behind the design, and drew out a sample quilt block. "See how there's a pattern to where the blocks are? Well, there's a pattern to the framing as well because it repeats."

She picked up a red pencil and quickly colored in a few spots. "By fitting pieces of cloth together like a puzzle, I create the stained glass window effect in the framing around the blocks. The photo squares are a white cotton poplin so they'll keep the true colors of the photos." She traded to a royal blue pencil and kept sketching as she talked. "The framing will be rich jewel tones, better than these pencils can do. The contrast between the vibrant color and the stark no color areas on the quilt create an opposite, like negatives to photos. That sets up the background for dimension. Then at set intervals, I'll add Crow beading designs for our heritage."

With a black pencil, Mara dabbed tiny circles into the design. "We may not live by hunting buffalo like our ancestors, but I want my children to know they have a beautiful ancestral line woven into their rich Irish heritage. Then the embroidered captions will have a theme running through the quilt to tell the story of Cadence's life. The beading adds dimension with patterns interspersed around the photos."

"If it's anything close to what I see here, this quilt is going to be a miracle in art. Quite an amazing piece of talent and skill." He took the notebook and turned it around a few different directions and studied her design. "I'm not artistic so I'll never get how ideas make it from a bunch of pictures to something that will look like that drawing. I hope I can see it all together one day."

She stared into blue eyes, not brown. Not at all like David's fiery, molten brown eyes. Blue like a cloudless Montana sky. Really, really nice eyes that had really, really nice smile lines around them. His eyebrows were darker than the wavy light brown hair he wore gelled back. They framed his blue, blue eyes so she couldn't take her attention away. Then he smiled at her and her heart flipped.

Mara ducked her head. It was nice to hear that Joel appreciated her artistic abilities for the sake of the beauty. David always saw her art as marketing materials. He always seemed to put a price on anything she created. Somehow she'd forgotten that little irritation. She'd forgotten she liked to create art with her hands simply for the sake of expression. She drew her brows together. When did she lose her love of art? Was it before David died or after, when she had to become everything to everyone?

She'd been sucked right into the design work before Joel arrived. It'd been three years since she'd used art for pleasure outside of work. The graduation quilt didn't start out about pleasure for herself. But as she watched Joel's fascination in her art, a little question formed. Would making this quilt from start to finish revive her joy, her love of creating for the sheer pleasure of creation?

"How do you come up with such intricate ideas?"

"I have a vision in my head." She tapped the pencil to her temple. "You know, I can see the finished product here. All I have to do is cut pieces of material to scale and sew them together. The photo memory quilt will be scrap pieces put together to depict windows of memories. I like the reversed idea that the stained glass effect makes up the vibrant framework like a relief to the snowy poplin. All these moments saved in pictures miraculously came together for

Cadence's life to be here and now and in this place. But you know, as her mom, I hope her life is filled with rich experiences into the future too. I'm creating a wish for her future in the symbolism of the border colors."

"How fitting. Our lives are woven together with what feels like scrap pieces. We can see clearly what's happened in the memories of our past. But the future, you're right. It's all hope, isn't it?" Joel looked directly into Mara's eyes. "You have a brilliant interpretation of God's design for Cadence's life in quilt art."

Startled by his response, Mara returned Joel's gaze in silence. The conviction behind his words shone from the depth of his soul. He believed wholeheartedly in God.

Did God take scraps and piece them together into beautiful art as she would do with this quilt? How did losing David fit in then? In that case, how did this man?

Joel picked up the pile of quilt blocks off the couch. He laid one out over his large hand. "Is this David?" The man stood next to a yellow and black snowmobile and wore a medal over his yellow and black winter gear. Louie sat at his feet with a yellow and black dog coat.

"Yes." Mara's stomach clenched at the

sight of the snowmobile. She hated, hated, hated that thing!

"By the look on your face, you didn't approve of his racing?"

She inhaled and closed her eyes. "It wasn't his racing. Although that should have been more than enough." She left the next thought unsaid. *How could I speak ill of the man I loved?* She blew out her breath with careful control. Still she fought for balance on this topic. They'd argued when he bought the dumb thing. He seemed to thrive on pushing more and more adrenaline through his body. He should have been a stuntman. "It was his risk-taking."

"Oh, I see."

"No, you don't. He won a lot of races. But they weren't enough. When extreme sports started getting popular, David took it to the next level. He and his buddies took their snowmobiles into the backcountry of the Bridgers. Then, according to the rescue patrol, they ignored the posted warnings."

She knew her voice took on an icy edge, but she couldn't help it. "He died because he was hill climbing on that machine and ended up racing ahead of an avalanche. But his avalanche beacon malfunctioned. It took them a long time to find him. When the guys dug David out, he was barely alive.

The snowmobile landed on top of him and created an air pocket. In fact, David lived almost two days after that. One lung had been crushed, several of his bones were broken, and the doctor said his spine was crushed."

"I can't imagine what you went though."

Tears choked her words, "He asked me to kiss him and let him go. He thought a man who couldn't walk, couldn't feed himself, and couldn't be a husband . . ." She reached for the glass of tea and sipped to relieve the clogged burning in her throat. "But I'd have rather had him here, walking or not." A tear rolled from her cheek and plopped into the glass. She set it back down, embarrassed. *Who cried in their tea?*

"Mara, I'm so sorry." Joel took her free hand in both of his. "Why would you put this photo on a quilt block when it causes you so much pain?"

"Cadence chose it. She wanted to remember him as strong and fearless. Not the broken man in the hospital."

"Ah, that makes a lot of sense."

"Joel, the nurses worked hard to clean him up enough not to scare the kids. The hard snowpack ripped his helmet right off. He was a mess. Bruises and scraped skin everywhere. His face was so raw I asked the nurses to cover David's face before the kids saw him. They couldn't even cast his arms and legs for all the open wounds. The nurse helped me hold a sheet above him to hide the worst from the kids." She looked at the photo. "I loved him so much. I can't believe he risked everything for a thrill. But he did, Joel, he did. And by doing that, he broke his promise to me. To our family. And God let him."

Joel moved closer to Mara and put his arms around her.

She cried there, safe against his shoulder. "God let him."

He pulled her in a little tighter. "That free will thing got me, too, for a while. After Sherice left, I went a little nuts. For some reason, I believed her betrayal proved there wasn't a God. I used that belief to keep distance between God and me." He rubbed a warm hand up and down Mara's back. "My anger at losing my wife, my ability to father children, and my dreams became the biggest excuse I had to avoid anything to do with the Lord."

"What do you mean excuse?" She sat up and pushed his arms away. Did he think she was making up excuses to avoid God? "There's a difference in excuses and reality, you know."

"I mean I used it as an excuse to avoid, like I said. I'd avoid friends, anyone who tried to comfort me with prayer or if they seemed like they were heading down that churchy path. I didn't want to pray to a God I didn't trust and I didn't want other people doing it either. So I ran hard and fast. I built my business ruthlessly."

He reached up and turned her face toward his. He held her cheek and brushed away a lingering droplet with his thumb. "That's when I tried to take over your company. Hostile takeover." He looked away. "The right words. I was downright hostile and I'm very sorry. I see now how damaging that was to you and your family. I took days out of your life with David I can't give back."

She opened her mouth to speak, but she couldn't say anything. Joel carried a weight too heavy for anyone. But she saw a little of herself in his confession.

"Can you forgive me?"

Mara raised a hand to cover his on her cheek. Was that how her friends and family saw her now? Hostile? Unavailable? Was she really making up excuses?

His warmth seeped into her frozen feelings. "You didn't take anything away from David and me. If it wasn't your business trying a move like that, it would have been another. We learned a lot. We both had, and I still have, gratitude for the lesson we learned in protecting our company."

"I'm forgiven?"

She smiled into those blue, blue eyes. Then she reached out and smoothed the wrinkles from his forehead. "Yes." How long did they sit there touching each other's faces? She wanted to trace his jaw, feel the shape of his bone structure, and lay her lips on his. She wanted something more than the emptiness of the last three years. The warmth of skin instead of the clammy feel of a leather chair. Maybe she was getting ready to get ready to date. A wisp of euphoria breezed across her mind.

"Mom!" Marisa's shout from the kitchen made them both jump. "Dinner's ready."

Mara pulled her hand back fast. She'd never meant to touch Joel in such an intimate way. Getting ready to get ready didn't mean she was ready. And definitely not with someone who needed to stay objective while coaching her. Had they crossed some sort of ethical line? "Dinner. Uh, yes." She nodded. "Coming," she called back.

"What's special about dinner tonight?"

The breezy euphoria turned back into a wintery gust. "Today is," she cleared her throat, "was, David's birthday."

Joel flashed serious right away. "Maybe I should go. I didn't know David or even how he died until you told me tonight. I'd be horning in on his family at a time focused on him." Joel moved to stand up. "I've done enough damage where that's concerned."

"No." Mara placed a firm hand on his knee. Joel's presence didn't feel as awkward now. But his leaving would. "The kids and I want you here."

"I don't know what to say or do for you."

Did she need to make him a cape? "Just normal everyday stuff, except for the birthday cake."

"Cake?"

"We bake a cake and sing happy birthday. Our family counselor suggested it as a way for the kids to understand they can still love and honor their memory of David." Did that sound a little over the top to him? Someone who didn't have kids maybe wouldn't understand. Or maybe this should be the last time they made such a big deal out of David's birthday. Maybe next year it should be a little smaller.

"Pretty smart counselor, if you ask me."

Mara smiled, "Thanks for understanding. Sometimes I think we're going a little overboard. But we miss him."

"M-o-m!"

8

Joel sat at Mara's desk a few days later and wondered about the intricate design work she could do with such patience and joy. Each night for the last week he had watched her nimble fingers embroider another quilt block. Her sense of fulfillment struck him. While she explained the quilt design, she never once noticed the time. Yet as they'd gone over the files and finances each night, she'd studied the clock on the wall or on her cell phone more times than he could remember. She could cipher the equations for the border patterns on the quilt without a twitch, but the number columns drove her to tension headaches. For Mara, when math created art it was magic. But the redundancies of multiple checks and balances to reveal various business nuances sparkled for Joel. If only they could be a team. Her creative abilities inspired him. Did anything about him inspire her?

After a meal with her family, Mara was lighter, happier, more relaxed. She loved spending time with the kids talking about their days, the dreams, and their friends. How did she not know she hated her job with such obvious opposites? For this company to succeed, Mara needed to love her job. Now he knew what she loved and what made her thrive: her family and art design. The shift had to happen to build on Mara's strengths. How could he help her shift her mind-set? But her stubborn strength of committed loyalty would be his mountain. Is this what the Bible means when it says your faith shall move mountains?

He rubbed the back of his neck. "Lord, I could use a lot of faith for this situation."

He placed a call to Rich. His mentor's perspective would help since he'd known Mara much longer and brought her up to speed when David died.

"How's it going up there in winter wonderland?"

"I tell you, Mara's keeping up with financials, payroll, and taxes from home on the laptop." Joel filled in his mentor and boss. "But Rich, I've noticed something and I'm not quite sure how to approach this with her."

"Well, let's talk it out."

"How is it that a woman as artistic, intelligent, and logical as Maria is can't see she hates her job?"

"Don't you think that's a little strong? How in the world did you determine she hates something she works at nonstop?"

"Rich, she's alive, vividly alive working on the quilt for her daughter."

"Of course she is. Every mother —"

"You don't get it. I sit with her every night and go over details from the day, reports, and future planning. She's a different person. Running the numbers, talking technical details seems to drain the life right out of her. She's like a cornered animal."

"How so, Joel?"

"She's attentive and thorough, don't get me wrong. But when I look at her doing numbers and reports, I see a woman whose every fiber of her being is screaming to be released from the trap. She loses her sense of joy. It's like watching a prisoner shovel load after load of gravel from one pile to another."

Rich's voice took on a fatherly tone. "Joel, are you getting a little too close?"

"Of course not," he stammered back. "I just think she could be, you know, I think she could be in a better position for her talents. It'd be good for the company overall if Mara's skill sets were lined up like all the other employees'."

"That's a good idea. I think you hit on the right plan."

"What's a good idea? What plan?"

"Let's have her take the tests all her employees take. David took the assessment test for the key management positions years ago. We only require one of the lead executives to test when we take on a company in mentoring. We'll find out if she's really suited to the position she's in or if you're reading into the situation."

"Right. Tell her she has to test now? Like she'll just jump on board."

"Joel, you're her coach now. I'm only here for a little while longer as you take on my full schedule. I'm already delaying my departure a few weeks due to the emergency up there. How are you going to know best what direction to guide her if you don't know who she is and what she's capable of?" Rich paused as he waited for Joel to catch up to his reasoning. "Joel, you need to know. Imagine the damage you'd do counseling her into areas she should delegate. Company CEOs that don't delegate appropriately set up their businesses to implode. Tell her that. I'm hoping she'll hear it from you."

Joel's head snapped up. He could convince Mara to take the online assessment tests in order to help him coach her to success and protect her company from implosion.

Rich continued, "My experience has been she's afraid to release control. She's worried if too much changes, it won't be the company David intended. Joel, you and I know even if David were still alive, the company would morph to survive. She can't hold it back and survive. Not in this economy. Help her learn to delegate and prepare an exit strategy or the entire company is at risk. What would happen if Mara were permanently disabled, not just dealing with a broken leg?"

"I'm with you."

They went over the progress since Mara's accident. Joel had the first week's training reports, a new CFO position description, and some new client design requests for her.

Rich suggested they pray over Mara, her business, and her family.

"Lord, all of this is for your purpose and glory. We ask you to open Mara's heart to receive wise counsel. Protect this company and build it to provide for all the employees and their families. We ask you to bless and grow Bridger Pack and Rescue so lives and souls may be saved. You have placed Joel in the right place at the right time to be your help in times of need. We ask you to be in all his actions and decisions as he helps the people you've put in his care."

"Thank you, Lord, for this awesome responsibility. Amen." Joel ended the prayer.

"Joel, I'm thinking you should extend another week in Bozeman before heading home to Denver. Help Mara settle into the shop's new expansion, prepare for new machinery deliveries, and meet the new employees. Your number-one goal is setting up a new chain of command for Bridger Pack and Rescue that allows Mara both an exit strategy and proper use of her skills and talents. Help her find people she can delegate and trust. Then get back here so I can golf!"

Joel chuckled at Rich's last line. He'd feel confident coaching by phone once all the daily procedures were in place with backup systems and he could turn the business back over to Mara. If something happened to Mara, there would be no leadership outside of a few shift leads. The company couldn't survive without Mara releasing some control to other key personnel. Then he'd be able to leave.

Joel frowned at the thought. He'd grown

used to the daily visits with the beautiful Mara Keegan. A warm home, dinner smells floating as he walked in the door each night, and the shouts of welcome. That's the life he thought he'd have. He'd miss her kids, too. Great kids, all three of them. It was probably just the Superman thing. Every man wants to be a hero. He smiled to himself. Thank you, Lord, for even this short time to know what it felt like to have a family. One more week to cherish that feeling, one more week to feel love, one more week and then he'd have to say good-bye. His jaw clenched. Joel realized he didn't want to say good-bye.

Joel punched the intercom. "Jill, please bring me the information on the company organizational chart."

First step, redistribute duties to others and free Mara up for more design work. Once he proved his hunch to her, they could put a new flow chart into action.

"I'm thinking you've got a bright idea, Joel," Jill said as she handed him the folder. "There's a light bulb hanging over your head."

He grinned up at her. "I do. And I think it would be much more successful if I could figure out a way to design it into a quilt."

Jill laughed, "Have you seen any of Mara's

quilt designs?"

"The one she uses while she sits on the couch and she's shown me the one for Cadence's graduation gift."

"Oh, wow, I saw that when I stopped by last week. Hoo whee, it's the most beautiful thing ever!" Jill turned to go, "You know what I think?"

"What?"

"I think we have almost everything we need to add a line of quilting design patterns. They can be sold online and to quilt shops. Maybe that's the next wall we leap, huh?"

Joel stared at Jill. "I think you are brilliant! You're also right. It can't happen yet with this large expansion, but it should be in the long-term planning. Thanks. I'll run it by Mara tonight at dinner."

Joel's mind whirled with the possibilities. They'd have to do some careful business planning, but adding another department to Bridger Pack and Rescue would set the company moving toward Solomon's advice in Ecclesiastes of seven streams of income. She'd have a stronger company if the revenue came through different streams. If one dried up, there'd still be six others flowing. He couldn't wait to see Mara's face when he told her Jill's idea.

With the chart in hand and an energized spirit, he started on the job description for a CFO position. In order for Mara's time to free up, she needed the financial management handled. The company was too big now, whether she liked it or not, to keep such a stranglehold on positions she could delegate. With Bridger Pack and Rescue up to forty-nine employees, payroll alone wiped out too many days in the month Mara needed to run her organization. She would cross the threshold to fifty employees with this new management position. His company would set up the larger accounting system and set a financial coach in place for the new chief financial officer. The skill, talent, and gifting assessment would be all he needed to convince Mara to run with it.

Tonight, they'd meet for dinner after Mara's first afternoon out of the house in over a week. She and the girls shopped for gowns for the Museum of the Rockies benefit ball next month. One more promise Mara refused to miss. Moments like this with her family took priority now that the doctor cleared her for short jaunts. Wouldn't it be nice to have a family to take priority? At least, he might give her more time with her kids.

He'd discuss the assessment results, the

newest client design requests, and the new CFO position over dinner with her tonight and get her to agree to a chief financial officer. If all went well, Mara's company would be positioned for a steep income increase over the next five years.

9

Marisa squealed, "This one!" She pulled out a long yellow gown. "Look, it has everything you're looking for."

"It's sure pretty, Marisa, but yellow?" Cadence shook her head. "I can't wear yellow. Off white, cream, something like that maybe."

"It was Daddy's favorite color."

"Yeah, it was." She took it and held it up to her chin in the mirror and then to her little sister's. "This color looks awesome on you though. So does the length. On me, it'd be way too short. We have to find the perfect shoes for this." The girls ran toward the changing room. "Be right back, Mom."

Mara found the chair outside the dressing area and sat down. She leaned her crutches against the wall behind her. Tired. She shouldn't have let her pride get in the way. The walker would have been much easier to maneuver. One store on crutches seemed to wear her out. She closed her eyes for the few minutes the girls were gone.

"Madame?" Cadence's voice cut through the sleepy fog.

Mara's eyes snapped open. She didn't realize how fast she'd fallen asleep.

"May I present to you, Miss Marisa Keegan." Cadence stuck her elbow out and escorted Marisa from the changing room. Then she twirled her around like a ballroom dancer. Mara thought of the old musicals like *Brigadoon* or *Seven Brides for Seven Brothers.* The dress billowed and swirled around Marisa. Both girls giggled until Marisa stopped in front of the three-sided floor-length mirror.

Mara watched her youngest gaze back from the mirror at Cadence with such adoration. She stood and stepped in to join them and pulled up the back of Marisa's hair. Cadence pulled a few strands down with her fingernails against the back of Marisa's neck. She held the rest of the heavy brown hair in a poufy bun.

Mara smiled, "Such an elegant young lady you've become. Are you Cinderella?" They all stood mesmerized for a moment by the vision in the mirror. Another moment would whisk by and Marisa would be graduating, too. Mara's heart squeezed a little.

"Mom's right, Marisa, you're really growing up." An older sister welcomed a little one over the threshold. She hugged her and then smoothed the sheer ruffled cap sleeve back in place.

At Cadence's words, Marisa blossomed. She lifted her shoulders back. The self-conscious child exuded the confidence of a debutante. In two ticks of a clock hand, Mara saw her youngest transform from a little girl playing at teen to a young lady teetering on womanhood. Two seconds. The Museum Ball wouldn't know what hit them when her lovely daughters made their entrance. Though the girls would work the coat check fund-raiser, they'd have the experience of dressing for the ball. Mara looked forward to watching her children gain the awareness of community generosity and working toward their own goals.

Cadence's dress became the next mission. Marisa hunted as if she tracked a bull elk in the Bridgers. The elusive perfect gown for her big sister would not get away. She surveyed the skirt colors around the bottom of the circulars. Then she whipped hangers aside as she rounded the next display. Around the tall racks, a whistle called to Mara and Cadence. "What did you find, GirlieQ?" Mara asked.

"Oh, Mom. Look!" Cadence gasped. The champagne-colored gown shimmered with an iridescent sheen. The bodice wrapped in tiny ruche pleats drew a visual to a small waist and the skirt swept down in a Grecian A-line.

"That's it." Mara fingered the chiffon material. "That's definitely you, sweetie."

"Come on, Marisa, you have to help me try it on." Cadence captured Marisa's hand and tugged her into the dressing room.

Long minutes later, Cadence appeared. While Marisa had morphed from little girl to pretty teen, Cadence emerged with an elegance that took Mara's breath away. The golden champagne enhanced Cadence's complexion to perfection. Her heart skipped a beat. When did this happen? When did both her daughters turn into such beauties so close to adulthood, so close to no longer needing her?

Mara felt tension build. She'd missed too much time at home working ridiculous hours. Being dad and mom and business owner meant she'd lost out on the daily time she used to have with her children. Children who weren't children anymore. Her chest tightened.

"You're beautiful, Cadence."

"Thanks, Mom." She dipped her head.

Her pleasure not quite hidden in the lowered posture. "It's way too long though. I think they make clothes for, like, Amazons." Cadence held up the skirt as she played with the length. "Wrong tribe," she joked.

Mara winked at her. "We can get it shortened." She motioned for Cadence to walk forward. She bent over in her chair and examined the amount of material. "What do you think about using some of this gorgeous material in your quilt? This dress is too pretty. And on you, well, I think it's one you'll remember for years to come."

"That would be totally awesome. What could you do with it?"

"Well, my first thought is to work it into the borders. Even with the amount we'd be able to cut, there'd only be enough for a few strategically placed pieces. But I might be able to highlight some special blocks if I used it as piping."

"Like outline it?" Suspicion clouded her face. "Won't that be one more chore?"

Tread easy here, girl. Mara sucked in a deep breath and nodded. "Very worth it if what I see in my mind turns out on your quilt. Or it could be some of the small stained glass pieces if I'm really careful. What do you think?"

When she looked up from the hem, Cadence beamed at her. "I'm liking that idea."

Warmth spread through Mara's body. Finally. There was the happiness, the connection, the chance to rebuild from the tension with Cadence. The whole afternoon gave Mara hope from the bubbly chatter to the humorous quips. Mara saw their relationship budding into something more than rebellious toleration.

"Time to find yours now, Mom." Marisa tugged on Cadence's arm to go change her clothes.

Marisa's fashion sense held true and she discovered the final gown. Red velvet, sweetheart neckline, sleek styling, pencil straight to the knee with a slight flare to the floor. A tiny triple pleat softened the back as it trailed from the hipline into a gentle short train.

The saleswoman noticed the crutches. "May I assist you?"

Mara loved it. "Do you have this in a size 6?"

"I do. Let me get it for you."

As soon as they were alone, Mara sat back down. "Girls, I think I need to rest. I'm feeling a little dizzy."

"Oh, Mom, I'm sorry. We just sprang you out too soon. You've gotta be whooped."

Cadence looked guilty. "Should we go home?"

"No, no. Let's just find a spot to get a coffee. I'll sit down and rest, okay?"

"Here we go, Ma'am. Should I put it in the dressing room?"

"I think if it's all right, I'm just going to take it." Mara pointed at her cast. "I can exchange it if it doesn't fit?" She'd be much more comfortable trying it on at home rather than trying to negotiate crutches and clothing.

"Absolutely. Let's get you all rung up." The saleswoman gathered all the hangers and slipped an arm under the heavy weight of three gowns. "Follow me and I'll have you set in a jiffy."

The crutches dug into her hands and side. Painful bruises battled with the pain of the broken ankle in Mara's mind. She didn't know which felt worse. Her ribs hurt, the heels of her hands hurt, and it must be hard work because she felt out of breath like she'd been running. A mist of fine perspiration broke out over her face and shoulders. "I think I'm getting a cold soda instead of coffee."

Marisa laughed, "You are getting a good workout, Mom. Even your face is all red."

The saleswoman pulled suit bags over the

lovely gowns with her back to the trio. "How would you like to pay?"

Marisa couldn't hold still. She'd slipped back into an excited little girl. Cadence leaned on the checkout counter and smiled as she watched Marisa practice dance steps. She reached out and swished the skirt of her dress.

Mara handed over a credit card. As they finished the transaction, Mara couldn't breathe. The pain in her neck felt sharper, more acute than the last time. She grabbed for air in gasps. The lights of the store beat down on her and spun as she went down.

"Call 9-1-1!" Cadence yelled.

"Mom!" Both girls dove toward her.

"Cadence," Mara moved her hand in the air. Cadence grabbed it.

"I'm here, Mom, I'm here."

"Call —" she gasped, "Joel." Then nothing.

Joel raced up to the sliding hospital doors. How long did it take for an automatic door to open? He slid through before it had fully retracted just as he had done at every stoplight on the way. For a small hospital, it seemed like precious seconds ticked away while he navigated the hall.

"Joel!" Marisa's full body wallop about

took him down.

Nothing mattered more in this moment than Mara and the kids. The huge world shrunk in his mind to four people. People who needed him as much as he needed them. He didn't want to think what it would feel like to lose Mara, to lose the sense of family he'd gained over the last two weeks. God, please help us.

"Hey, honey." He kept his voice low, but wrapped her in a fatherly hug. "How's your momma?" She didn't look thirteen. Through her tears, she looked like a scared three-year-old.

"I don't know. They won't tell us anything."

Cadence stood behind Marisa. "We've been waiting to hear something, but they —" Her voice cracked and she stopped. "The paramedics said she was having a heart attack! Joel, is she going to —"

Joel captured Cadence's gaze and shook his head in quick spurts. He tilted his eyes at Marisa. "Hey, let's hold that thought." He held out an arm. Cadence dove against his side. He folded her into his embrace. "Okay, gals, sometimes the best thing we can do is pray and wait." He lowered his chin against the top of Cadence's head. "Anybody get hold of Toby?"

"Yeah." Cadence nodded. Her hair stuck in the stubble of his chin as she pulled away to look up at him. "His buddy's bringing him over from basketball."

"Dude!" Toby greeted them with a grim face from down the hall. He wore a black hoodie, hood up, over long basketball shorts. His hands burrowed into the front center pocket. He jogged toward them, "Is Mom okay?"

"We haven't heard anything yet, Toby." Joel noticed all three kids crowded in as close as possible. The girls hadn't left his hug. If anything, they held on tighter. "Is this where they want us to wait?"

Cadence answered, "Yeah, the nurse said someone would come to talk to us if we stayed here."

He tipped his head toward the chairs in the corner. "Come on, guys, let's sit down over there."

He chose the corner chair and let the kids fill in around him. They pulled their chairs into a tight semicircle. At this moment, he was their anchor. They needed someone much bigger than one Joel Ryan to anchor them if this didn't turn out well. If Mara . . . Joel's gut twisted at the thought of Cadence, Toby, and Marisa alone. His mouth went dry. Mara had to survive! He didn't know what he'd do if . . . Joel caught himself. *No, not going there.* He scanned the kids' worried faces. "We have to take this to the Big Guy."

Marisa stared at her crossed feet. "Do you think he really cares? He probably decided already." She looked up with huge tears spilling onto freckled cheeks. "He didn't save my dad. Why would he save my mom?"

Joel thumbed away the tears as he took Marisa's petite face in both hands. "Not only does he care, but no one said we've lost your mom. Prayer is powerful."

He saw Toby's doubt, Marisa's fear, and Cadence's sense of defeat. "It's like the best basketball games. Both teams are fighting hard to score all the way to the end. It keeps the tension up and everyone interested in the game. We're going to mount the best offense because we have a wise coach who already knows the outcome. He's calling us into the huddle where we ask him what to do and he directs the plays."

Did he go overboard here? Did the kids catch the idea or should he try again? He'd never acted the part of family anchor before, as a father would. Right here, right now, he wished he could be a father. No, not just a father. He ached for these kids, loved these kids. Loved their mom. His eyes widened.

He raised his head from his own contemplation to see if he'd given anything away. None of them seemed to notice anything beyond the conversation.

Toby turned to Marisa. "I bet the Big Guy coaches a great defense too."

Joel smiled. "I hear he's the best there is."

Cadence nodded. "Okay, so huddle already."

Somehow, they managed to close any hint of distance as the chairs scraped closer. Toby lifted his arms and put one around his younger sister, then the older. The girls responded by wrapping their arms around Toby and Joel. Joel joined them, completing the circle with his arms. Anyone walking by would see a team huddle.

"Do you think God minds you calling him Big Guy when you talk about him?" Marisa asked. She'd stopped crying.

Joel shook his head. "Nope. I think he knows exactly who he is and it helps me remember he's a lot bigger than I am. I've got no power here," he pulled a hand back for a moment and thumbed toward the heavens, "but the Big Guy does."

"Then I'm calling him that too." Marisa took Joel's hand and squeezed.

Joel squeezed back. "Huddle?"

The rest all responded together,

"Huddle!"

A small giggle spurted out of Marisa. "So, how do you actually pray? Like what do you actually call God?"

Joel's smile spread across his face. "Just like this." He bowed his head, "Dear Big Guy . . ."

Marisa giggled, followed by a little sniffle.

Joel winked at her and started again. "Dear Big Guy, we're scared. We bring ourselves to you to pray for help to protect Mara. Mara is sick and needs your healing hand to wake up and be healthy for her children. There's nothing we can do on our own, but you've brought us together as a team to send up prayers for her. Please guide the doctors, nurses, and medical staff. Help them to use the miracle of science, and where science fails, send a miracle. Please bring her back to our family. In Jesus' name, Amen."

Marisa's head popped up. "You said *our* family."

"Yeah, you did, Joel." Cadence backed up Marisa.

Joel's mouth went dry. He hadn't meant to say it. "I think it's just natural, you know. I couldn't think of how else to say it without a lot of words."

Toby didn't say anything, but his eyes bee-lined into Joel's.

Now what?

10

"Hey there," Joel whispered near Mara's shoulder. "Guys, she's waking up."

Marisa jumped up from her chair to grab Mara's hand. "Mommy, I was so scared."

Cadence put her hand on Marisa's shoulder. "Hi Mom." Her face looked drawn and worried.

Mara tried to blink away gritty eyes and focus on her kids. But a mouse lifting a house might have a better chance since that's about the strength she had.

Toby unwound from the maze of chairs stuffed around her bed, but stayed seated. "Dude, you look like you were hit by a truck." He had a sweet, gentle grin.

"Dude?" She croaked out. "Dude?" They all laughed softly at her weak smile. "I'm tired." She coughed a bit and closed her eyes.

"We'll let you rest, sweetie. It's so good to know you woke up for a minute," Joel soothed her. "I'll call a nurse to let them know Sleeping Beauty returns." He winked at her.

She smiled at him through her lashes. She didn't have the energy to fully open her eyes.

"You guys want a sandwich?"

Three gentle kisses on her cheek. She sighed. Except for the "dude," she'd think they were a dream. Mara forced herself to crack her eyelids to prove they were real. He was there. Joel was right there being strong for her children as he shepherded them out the door. Her eyes slipped closed again. *Sweetie* floated around her dreams.

The hospital cafeteria brimmed with people. Familiar with the food line and layout after dinner last night and this morning's breakfast, all four separated to their favorites and met up again at the register. Joel pulled out his wallet and paid for lunch.

"Thanks again," Cadence said. "You've taken great care of all of us since last night. I know my mom is really going to appreciate it."

"Yeah, you're a pretty cool dude," Toby joined in.

Marisa added a sweet thank-you.

"I'm glad to. Come on." Joel held a tray loaded with soup, sandwich, two peanut butter cookies, and a tea. He motioned with his elbow. "Let's grab that table over by the far wall."

Under Joel's leadership, the kids lifted trays full of food and followed him in a line. They'd eaten very little since the day before. Even Toby's appetite hadn't been up to his normal scarf-down. Marisa had flicked her rice by the grain from one side of her plate to the other last night. A few times onto his hand or like Velcro bombs onto Toby's glass. He hoped the hospital's lunch special, spaghetti and garlic toast, would disappear — into her stomach today. Cadence hadn't even bothered to try. She'd sipped on a latte to keep herself awake at her mother's side after a night of no sleep. Her tray loaded with beef stew and salad said hope had returned.

If the kids had been able to see Mara before the surgery, it might have helped them settle down some. But then again, he hadn't seen her condition. It might have been worse. Joel sent up a prayer of thanks that the medical staff made every effort to bring in the kids once she'd been moved from recovery and that the kids pulled him in with them. This small town seemed to have a much more personable attitude with a little flex when needed. Joel didn't know what he'd have done if the hospital rules kept the kids away from their mom any longer than necessary. It helped that many of the same people still worked in emergency that were here when Mara's husband died. They seemed to know the family.

When they were all seated, Marisa asked, "Joel, could we huddle again? I felt a lot better after that." She choked up. "And Mom woke up just like you prayed. Maybe she'll heal faster if we keep praying."

"Sure." He bowed his head. The three teens did too. "Lord, we're all asking you to turn your eyes on us and listen to our prayers. Thank you for your healing hand on Mara. Please continue to heal her and ease her recovery. Help us to be available in whatever way you need us to be for her too. We also thank you for providing this food to nourish and strengthen us. In Jesus' name."

Marisa closed the prayer, "Amen." She twirled her fork in a little circle as pasta swirled into a big ball. "I liked it better when you called him Big Guy." She stuffed a giant ball of noodles and sauce into her mouth.

Joel laughed. "I'll remember next time." Marisa looked happy as she sat spinning another forkful. As busy as she always seemed until Mara's collapse — maybe the word was *bouncy* — she relaxed and ate in peace. Prayer poured peace over this family.

An older couple walked up to their table. "I hope you don't mind us stopping to say something," the woman said, "but we have seen your family down here a few times. Virgil and I thought it was nice to see you all pray, but the prayers must be working. Your bunch seems cheery today. It's so encouraging to see families praying together and God answering prayer."

Joel started to correct them, but Cadence cut him off. "Thank you, ma'am. Our mom had heart surgery and she's waking up more. The doctor says she's going to be okay."

"Virgil, did you hear that?" She leaned into his ear and repeated the situation. "What good news!"

"Yes, yes, good news." Her husband chimed in clapping Joel on the back. "You sure have done a good job with these young 'uns."

"Oh, I —"

Marisa jumped in this time, "He's pretty great. He's our Superman!"

Virgil turned to his wife, "What'd she say?"

The woman raised her voice, "She said

he's Superman, Virgil, Superman."

Everyone in the near vicinity turned and looked at their table. Joel couldn't remember turning red ever in his life. His face heated up like a fireplace.

He smiled and nodded. "Good thing to like your dad like that," Virgil said.

"Oh, that's the way it should be. Dad should be the hero." His wife leaned in toward the table again. "We just wanted to say watching your family has helped us as we wait for news on our son. His name is Eric. We came down for his chemo and he ended up in critical care. Would you pray for Eric and we'll pray for your mom? What's her name?"

"What are you saying, Bess?"

She raised her voice again, "We're trading prayer requests with Superman's family, dear."

"Her name is Mara." Joel tried one more time. "I'm just a friend, though."

"Just a friend? Really? You fit in so well with these kids we were positive they belonged to you."

"They're sure easy to hang out with." He gave the kids a wink and smile.

"Where's their dad?"

Cadence answered, "Ma'am, he died a few years ago in an accident."

"Oh, my. Well, maybe you should be together."

"What, Bess?"

She shook her head. "No daddy. They belong together, right?"

"Oh, yes, yes."

"Your Mara, she's in our prayers, too, then." They shook hands with each of the kids and Joel and then left the cafeteria.

"That was funny," Marisa giggled. "They thought you were our dad." She ripped opened a packet of Parmesan cheese and shook it on a portion of her spaghetti.

"Well, I think we should have corrected them sooner. But sometimes it's not as important to be right as it is to be present and meet the need." Was God sending a message by sending the elderly couple? Joel tried to get the sandwich to go down, but had to reach for his tea. His throat seemed a bit constricted all of a sudden. Did God have more than business in mind by sending him to Montana? Besides the fact that he'd always wanted to be a father, enjoyed the mini support role he played for the time being, and seemed to be in the kids' good graces at the moment, he'd been around enough to know stepparenting had its own complications.

"Yeah, but you know what?" Marisa tasted

the pasta. With a mouthful she said, "I wish you were."

Joel barely kept from spitting the tea. He started to cough as the drink went down the wrong tube.

"You all right, dude?" Toby pounded his back.

"I think we'll need to just take things one step at a time. Okay?"

All three nodded but Marisa piped in, "Sure. I already prayed about it so I'm not worried. God answered our prayers for Mom. He'll answer mine too."

"Marisa!" Cadence scolded. "I was being nice to those old people. I like Joel, too, but you can't make Mom and Joel, like, fall in love or something."

Toby spoke up as he shoveled chili and cheese onto a nacho chip. "Well, it wouldn't be a bad thing. I'm gettin' tired of being the only guy in the house. It's girl stuff, girl movies, girl talk all the time. Man, another guy would be cool." He opened wide and chomped the entire heavy-laden chip. "But Cadence is right. They gotta figure it out without us messing it up."

Joel leaned forward, "Tell you what, guys, I really like your mom but how about we get everyone through the next few weeks before we go making any plans? She has a long way to go right now and doesn't need a lot of extra pressure. Deal?"

They chorused a round of "Deal."

Marisa's knowing smile sent a light whisper through his spirit. *Is this what you have planned, God? If it is, you're going to have to really make it plain and simple.*

Joel's heart swelled at the acceptance from the Keegan kids. They trusted him, needed him, and might love him as much as he was learning to love them. He'd call in to the main office and make arrangements for the next few weeks as Mara recovered. He knew the timing that placed him in Bozeman wasn't a fluke. Three confirmations in one day? His own thoughts, the couple thinking they were a family, and the discussion with the kids.

Lord, I'll be here as long as they need me and you want me here, but like I said, please make it clear. Have you prepared a place for me in this family? Do they need me as much as I seem to want to need them?

The nurse gave Joel five minutes and Jill acted as the witness as Joel read the power-of-attorney to Mara. He hated waking her up, but without her signature, all fifty employees were going to miss paychecks in the morning. "All this is going to do is allow

151

me to handle the business until you're able to take over again. It has to be renewed after the ninety-day expiration." Mara nodded off again.

Jill touched her shoulder. "Mara? Can you handle just a few more minutes? I promise we'll take care of everything for you and make you proud."

She opened her eyes. "Sorry, I'm just so tired." Her voice held the rasp still from the tubes during surgery. "They're going to make me sit up in a chair tomorrow and then start walking. Hobbling really."

"I know." Jill held her hand. "You've had a ton of challenges. We're going to share some of those with you while you recover."

Joel listened to the sweet way Jill encouraged Mara. She had good friends, good doctors, and a good life ahead of her. Would she need him in it? The question surprised Joel. Then he couldn't stop wondering. She looked so fragile. He knew he had to set the new plan in motion more than ever to help her. "We need to get payroll out though. I don't think you're up for signing checks quite yet. If you'll sign here, I can do that for you until you're up and about."

She took shallow breaths. Joel's chest constricted with empathy. *God help her. She looks so broken.* "Are you up for this or should we come back?"

"Yes, I know we need to do this." She dropped the pen he gave her. Jill bent to pick it up and then handed it to Mara. She signed, but it took a lot of energy. Her hand landed back on the bedside table.

Jill lifted Mara's hand and tucked it under the blanket. "I think we should let her sleep."

The nurse stood nearby. "There's a lot of medicine in her system to get her through this." She waited to walk both of them out to the station. "She's had a hard day, but you wait and see how fast she improves. We don't let our patients laze around."

"If you did, she wouldn't anyway." Jill smiled. "Not Mara, not with her driven personality."

Joel walked out with the women. At the door, he turned and looked back at Mara. She may be type A, but she couldn't do this solo anymore. He'd do everything he could to give her a solid company and the freedom to create.

"Mom?" Toby's voice came from the other side of the curtain. "You decent?"

Mara took a deep breath. Talking still took a lot of energy even two days out from surgery. The forced coughing to clear her lungs kept her throat a tad sore. "Sure, honey, as much as I can be."

He slid the hospital curtain back enough to come inside. "How ya' doin'?"

She held out her hand and he took it. "I've been better. Seems like all your grandpa's horses trampled me, though." Mara motioned for Toby to hover in for a hug. "How are you doing?" Three years and a few weeks after he lost his father, he nearly lost his mom. Fifteen. Toby needed time to grow up before more tragedy hit. Emotion choked in Mara's throat. Her children could be orphans. Then what?

He shrugged, but his face looked drawn and pale. "I was kinda worried."

She cleared her throat to rid herself of the clog there. "I'm sorry I scared you, Toby. This has to be really rough. Are you eating, honey?"

"Yeah, Joel's been takin' care of that."

"I'm so grateful." Joel the coach. Joel the kid handler. Would he be upset with all the demands? "He's done so much for us."

"Grandma is here. She'd have been here sooner but they shut the airport yesterday from the blizzard." He smiled. "She said she was coming this time whether you wanted her or not. Joel went to get her at the airport."

"He did, did he?" This would be interesting. Her mother never thought she should be running the company. She wanted her to pursue her art. Would she harp on that and say the business caused her heart attack? Or would she assume Joel was her new beau?

"Marisa and Cadence went with him." He sat a little closer. "I told them I'd hold down the fort."

Mara's heart rate picked up. Mrs. Calder called to say hello this morning. Wasn't she holding down the fort? "Who is with you at home? Are you guys getting your homework done?"

"Mom, we're good. Honest. Joel's staying next door at Mrs. Calder's house now." He started to snicker. "She told him that's what was happening because she knew you'd want him around in case of emergency for us. She made us all program his number into our cells."

"Back up. He's what?" Mara didn't know what to think. Now Joel was managing her children at home too? Too much.

"No worries, Mom, he's been cool. He made sure we called Grandma and he took us out for dinner last night. And you'll love this, he made us all go to school today, too, or I'd have been over sooner. He said you had work to do so we did too."

She started to laugh, "Oh, oh. Ow. I can't do that." She held her hand over the stitches. "School. That sounds like torture."

"Yeah, and Grandma already gave Cadence the third degree about him."

That comment brought Mara's undivided attention. "What do you mean?"

"Well, after he called her —"

"Who called her?" Mara tried to push herself up to sitting. "Joel called her?" She couldn't talk and sit up at the same time yet. Toby leaned over and helped her up. "How did he know to call her?"

"He asked. You were in surgery and we didn't know . . ." Toby's voice trailed off.

Mara still held Toby's shoulders. She pulled him close. "Oh Toby. I'm sorry. I'm so sorry you had to go through that."

He wriggled out of her arms. His voice thick with emotion, "I'm glad you're here, Mom."

"Me too." She smiled. "Oh, me too, honey."

Toby brushed his long brown hair back off his face with both hands. "I'll go see if they're here yet. They left right after you fell asleep."

God, since you decided not to take me, how about a little help with a speedy recovery? My kids need me. You've already got one of us.

It's the least you could do, right?

Even with the miracle of her life, God felt so far away. But she hadn't been exactly trying to build a relationship with him either. As Toby walked out of the room, Mara had the feeling God hadn't been the one to leave her alone. She'd been the one to walk away from him as easily as Toby disappeared through the door in search of Grandma.

Hugs, hugs, and more hugs. "Okay, Mom, I'm okay. But I won't be if you keep squeezing me to death." She took her mother's hands and held them. "It hurts to hug right now." It hurt to see her mom's reaction as tears welled up in her eyes.

"Mara, I've been a mess trying to get here to you. Who'd have thought Phoenix would be so difficult?"

"I'm glad you made it." She meant it. Her mother's comfort and solid good sense would help her through the next few weeks. As a retired nurse, Beth O'Reilly's healing hands and knowledge would be a blessing. And she wouldn't have to fully rely on Joel.

"If your daddy were alive, I think he'd have driven me all the way here, snow or no snow."

"I know. I'm impressed you managed to get up here so fast. Toby told me there was another blizzard." Her parents moved down to Sun City, Arizona, when their first grandchildren came along from her older brother. Once Mara's children arrived, they'd split their time with winters in Arizona and summers in Montana. Beth continued on for the last five years after her husband died in order to share time with all seven grandchildren.

Beth moved her hands to Mara's cheeks. "I just needed to see you and know you're okay." She leaned down and kissed the indentation at her temple as she had when Mara was a toddler.

Mara turned her face more deeply into the comfort of her mother's palm. "I love you, Mom," she whispered.

11

"I see you have your laptop here." Vickie, the hospital social worker sat by Mara's bedside. "Are you planning to work?"

She looked over at the MacBook Pro. "I need to as soon as I can." Mara leaned back on her pillow. "Somehow I've got to get my financials done. I don't have the energy yet, though. They've kept me hobbling the halls and working on my breathing treatments. I can't do the stairs yet with this cast, and by the time I'm done with it all, I just want to rest."

"We have to get you freed up when you go home so you have the ability to recover and rest. Who is someone who can step in for a few weeks?"

"There's no one."

"Really? No one?"

Mara's thoughts went to the one person who'd proved himself trustworthy, capable, and knowledgeable enough to run her company. He'd been running it without her. And that was the last thing she wanted from someone who couldn't stay. "I don't have anyone I can ask."

Joel managed to handle the day-to-day operations while she kept up with the financials from home. If only he could be part of her permanent team. She missed sharing the load with David. But Joel had a job and a life of his own. This was her cross to carry. "I mean I've asked too much already. I can't ask him to do more."

"Let's think this through. You can't or you won't?" Vickie's eyes stayed trained on Mara. "If you don't take time to heal, what will happen?"

Mara bit her tongue. She didn't want to say his name out loud. He'd already given two weeks of his life. Two weeks she couldn't give back. Two weeks more indebted. Her children already relied on him and it seemed her mother was falling fast for him, too. Every time she visited, she sang his praises. Mara had to agree with her observation of Joel's father-like relationship with her kids. She had to do something about that before her children were hurt.

"Since this someone's been able to help in the past, wouldn't he be willing to help now?"

Mara turned to look at the woman. "Yes, but I've already asked too much of him."

"How do you know? Have you asked him how he's feeling about helping you?"

"No."

"Then how can you possibly know what someone else is thinking?"

"But —"

"Mara, assumptions are brick walls you build around your heart. You mean well. But those walls make it impossible to see outside of your own ideas. Walls without windows don't give you the chance to see the view." She held up a finger to stay Mara's rebuttal. "Walls built to keep people out. That's a very lonesome and stark existence."

Mara turned to look out the window, glad of the beautiful view of mountains, sky, and billowy clouds. "It's the way it is right now."

"May I ask you to consider your children?" The clouds slipped across the sun and shadows filled the room.

Low blow. She turned back to Vickie. "I am." She thought of little else but the legacy she and David had built for their family and the families who worked for them. What would happen if they became more attached to Joel? More reliant on him? No, she needed to protect all of them from unreasonable expectations and she could not put more expectation and responsibility on someone that should be mentoring her by phone and at annual meetings for long-term business planning.

"If you don't take the time to recover, Mara, what happens when the next heart attack or a stroke happens?"

"That's why I had the surgery. To correct the problem."

The social worker tented her fingers and pulled them up to her lips. "How are you feeling today, Mara?"

She closed her eyes. Not as bad as David must have. She saw him lying in the hospital bed again. She felt him close as if three years hadn't passed. "Not good." Did she look as bad? Was she imprinting horrible memories on her children?

"Mm. How long do you think it'll be before you're feeling better?"

Questions. Tons of questions. She should open her eyes, but it felt better to lie still and quiet.

"Mara?" The thick compassion in Vickie's voice and the gentle hand placed across her arm drew Mara's attention.

She sighed. "I don't know."

"This is day four. The doctor wants to release you tomorrow. But he doesn't feel comfortable doing that unless we have a plan in place to help you."

Oh my goodness. Joel's time in Bozeman wasn't two weeks. It was nearly three. Why did he stay? He must be putting his own job in jeopardy as he protected Bridger Pack and Rescue for her. David faded away. No. Was he doing it for her or because there was no one else? She could have Jill bring anything she needed to the house. Her mother could help her arrange some sort of schedule for rehab and work.

"Listen, I'm not trying to stonewall you here. But I really don't have anyone who can do what I do. He needs to go home." Her own words sounded hollow, forlorn. *I really don't have anyone.* She fought back the burn in her throat as she sought the window again.

"Then we need to find a solution."

Joel poked his head in the door and knocked on the door-jamb. "Am I intruding?"

"No." Mara forced a weak smile. *Sure, show up when I'm trying not to need you. You're like the fish I kept catching and trying to throw back.* "This is my business coach, Joel."

The social worker smiled and then stood. Mara noticed a sense of confidence about the woman. "Why don't you two visit for a short time and we'll take a break. Mara, I'll come back in a little bit. Maybe your coach here might have some suggestions." She nodded at Joel with a meaningful look and stepped out of the room.

Great. With a polite introduction, Mara opened a conversation she didn't want to have with Joel.

"What's all that about?" Joel asked. He walked to the chair on the opposite side of the bed the social worker vacated. Then he pulled it a little closer than it had been. His eyes held question and compassion — and something more.

Swim, fish, swim. "Nothing out of the ordinary." Mara put as much indifference in her voice as she could. "We're working on my discharge plan."

"That's fantastic news!" Joel's face lit up. He squeezed her hand then didn't let go.

He leapt for the hook and it wasn't even in the creek. She turned her head away and covered a yawn. "I can't wait to go home. I feel like I get woken up here every couple of hours." She flicked her free hand toward the door. "It's cold and noisy and everybody's always after me to do something, eat something, drink something, climb something. I've never felt more bullied in my life!" With that she dropped her head back on the pillows plumped behind her back. According to the social worker, she wouldn't be going anywhere until she had a plan in place. She grimaced.

"What was that grimace for? Are you in pain?"

She sighed. "Fine, fine." She might as well tell him. She lifted her head from the nest of pillows. "The plan has to include time off work or the doctor won't let me go home."

"You thought it would be different?" He chuckled.

"Oh, come on, Joel. They want several weeks. You know as well as I do that's impossible." She looked down at her hand and back up at him. The warmth from his gentle grip comforted her as his thumb rubbed across her knuckles, almost as if peace seeped from him and into her. But she needed to throw this fish back. Mara tugged her hand back.

"Not so impossible. I'll help you figure it out." Their gazes locked.

She did not want Joel solving every problem. He had his own life and needed to go home. But this one seemed bigger than her. In fact, everything seemed too big right now. She wished he could stay. A shoulder to sink into when she felt low wasn't a good enough reason to ask when the shoulder belonged to someone who couldn't stay, wouldn't be in her life. "I just . . . I need some rest."

Her voice trailed off as she fell asleep. Joel hung his head. She wasn't up to all the new business details. Another time. He stood and then made his way quietly out of the room. He took a last glance at her. She looked pale on the pillow, so weak. "I'm here for you, Mara. I'm really here."

The social worker waited at the nurse's station. "Joel?"

"Yes." He smiled and held out a hand. "Joel Ryan."

She shook his hand. "How'd it go in there?"

He tilted his head toward her room door. "She's resting."

"Did she make any decisions?"

"She mentioned the doctor required several weeks off work. But I think we have a hardhead in there."

"Let me ask you something." She directed him over to the alcove. The small room held a TV and a few chairs. Once seated together at a corner table, she offered the information. "Joel, as a coach, how can you help her release work to recover?"

"Easier than you think, actually," Joel offered. "But I need to know what the doctor and you need to happen."

"I can tell you this much. Mara must have the time for physical therapy, exercise, and follow-up appointments. It's impossible for her to focus on work during the first few weeks after release from the hospital. She seems to feel she can't ask for help. Do you know a way we can get through to her so she doesn't jump the gun and race off to work before she's ready? She sure doesn't need a relapse."

Joel's mind raced. *Lord, I was already prepared to stay. Guide me here.* "How long does she need to fully recover?"

"The doctor feels she'd fully recover in four to six weeks. She can return to work slowly with a graduated raise in hours. Without sufficient recuperation, she'll relapse and struggle."

"I understand." Four weeks, maybe six. It'd take some hefty rearranging after the three he'd already been away from the office. "I can do that for her. I'll work it out and extend for as long as she needs me."

She patted his hand. "Joel, you really care about Mara. Don't you?"

He choked. "Of course."

"I don't mean like a friend." She leaned

in and looked into his face. "Ah, I see. You know you care." She sat back in her chair. "But she doesn't?"

12

The social worker's words haunted Joel all night and ran through his brain on the way to the office the next morning. If it was so easy to see how he felt, did Mara suspect? Is that why she seemed so standoffish at his visit?

Jill buzzed in on the intercom. "Rich's on the line for you."

"Rich, this is a surprise. I planned to call Denver this afternoon."

"How is Mara doing?" Joel heard a fatherly tone in his friend's voice.

"Great, considering. The doctor let us take her home this morning, so it's a bit of a late start at the shop today. Her mom will be here for a week or so to help out."

"Good to hear. I've been praying for her and the kids. She sure has some great kids, doesn't she?"

"I haven't met teens I like more," Joel agreed. "I may be a little partial."

Rich didn't respond right away. "Listen Joel, there's no easy way to say this." Another uncomfortable pause turned the conversation. "We need you to come on back as soon as you can. The hotel costs are mounting."

"Rich, I know it's been more than we expected, but I can't leave Mara at this point. Her neighbor, Mrs. Calder, asked me to stay at her house a few nights ago. I'll be happy to take over the rental car cost as I'm choosing to stay. That should take care of the expenses."

"Let me put it another way. You're becoming too enmeshed in the situation. We have other clients who deserve your attention, too."

"I've agreed to make sure she's freed up for physical therapy and follow-up appointments. She has weeks of recovery left. It's not possible to train someone to come in and be the company head for a month."

"Joel, that's my point. Our last discussion was about getting the management system set in place. Now I have to ask, is it the company you can't leave or Mara?" Rich didn't mince words. "At this point, you should have a fairly good management crew. Do you or are you delaying for some other reason?"

His mouth worked, but no sound came out. Rich was the second person in one day to drive straight to the heart of the matter. How could it appear so obvious to both a stranger and a close friend when he hadn't told anyone how he felt? On the surface, it should look like an emergency solution.

Joel realized he'd been silent too long. "Rich, yes, I'm working on it. I've hired a new CFO. She's in training now. But there hasn't been any time to handle all of it yet. Mara still hasn't had a chance to meet Constance let alone approve the position. Constance is on a ninety-day trial period, more for the opportunity to get Mara on board."

"This is exactly the scenario we've been trying to help her understand since David died. She has to have an exit strategy built into her business plan. The business will crumble without someone already being trained."

Joel was still back in the last question. Was he delaying the process because he didn't want to leave Mara? He saw her on the ground in her home workshop, her hair splayed across the floor. He saw her smiling as she designed Cadence's quilt. He loved the sparkle in her eyes as she greeted him each night when he arrived with the day's report from the shop. His gut clenched at the memory of nearly losing her. How happy it made him to see her alive after the emergency call from Cadence.

Joel's heart soared as he thought of the moment she woke up in the hospital after surgery. It wasn't the business that kept him here or the fear of failure. It was a strong woman who had a penchant for challenging life itself. But until she made peace with God and David's memory, Joel couldn't consider a relationship. She needed time and so did he.

"Did you hear me?"

"Sorry, what?"

Rich's voice grew stern. "Joel. Exit strategy. Focus on getting it finished for both your sakes."

Joel hung up as Jill brought in the newest applications and a basket of fruit.

"Hey," she smiled. "I wondered if you'd mind delivering this when you take the daily reports by Mara's house? I know she's home now, but I'm not thinking she's up to a bunch of visitors parading through her living room yet."

"Sure, no problem."

"If I keep sending fresh fruit, maybe she'll start eating right. I've tried to get her to eat fruits and veggies over the last few years.

Goodness knows, I've tried to get her to just slow down and eat lunch more than once a week."

"What do you mean?"

"You have to know Mara by now. She's type A all the way. After she promised David in the hospital that she'd make this business succeed, she went from eight-hour days to twelve with no lunches. When the kids are gone on ski trips or to camp, I don't think she goes home. I have to bring something in and stick it right under her nose. Sometimes I even hold her calls so she'll eat the sandwich."

"No wonder she had a heart attack." He shook his head. "It's a good thing she had you to at least hold the calls."

"Oh no, she didn't. I did it. And don't you ever tell her. I need a secret weapon to take care of her, you know?"

"Yes, I do." They shared a conspiratorial laugh. "She is one power house, isn't she?"

"And that's an understatement." Jill laughed. "But look what she's been able to do up until now. I think the only thing keeping her halfway healthy are the workouts she does a few times a week. She used to work out, run, and even ski all the time. Now . . ." She shrugged.

"Jill, I need something from you."

"What's that?"

"I need you to help me build up a support system around Mara so she doesn't have to die to achieve her goals."

Jill stepped back toward his desk. A curious expression crossed her features. "How are we going to do that?" She sat on the opposite chair and rubbed her palms together as if waiting on a delicious morsel. "Do tell."

"We're going to put people in strategic positions to free up Mara from financials, human resources, and floor supervision. She's been doing too many jobs that can be reassigned to help the company run more effectively. The plan is to have a daily system of oversight, but give her designing and publicity time."

"I get it," Jill blew out a long breath. "But she's going to thrash you." Jill drew out the last two words as she grinned at him.

"Not when she takes on more in her real talents. She'll be able to act as the spokesperson, the face of Bridger Pack and Rescue and still hold all final decision power. Everyone else will do the work and report to her as it should be for a CEO. Mara will feel alive, involved, and more fulfilled. With a team in place, the best benefit is that she'll be able to work normal hours and not carry the entire load by herself."

Jill raised an eyebrow as she stood. "I agree with you in theory." She turned toward the door and tossed a comment over her shoulder, "And I'm going to get rich selling tickets to the show when you tell her."

"Jill," Joel called after her, "are you in?"

She stopped at the door and turned back with a grin as big as Montana's wide sky. "Oh yeah, I am so in!"

Mara watched Louie from her recliner. "I heard the car, did you, boy?" He seemed a little less enthusiastic than normal and like he'd lost some weight, no raised head, but his tail wagged. "We're both on the outs today, huh? Guess we pushed it a little hard." He wagged his tail a little harder. "I'll make sure you get some extra treats from now on. How's that?" His tail thumped.

A light rap on the door, Joel opened it. "Hey, how's the miracle lady?" He brought Jill's fruit basket with him.

He set it down on the coffee table within reach for Mara but not in the way of her foot pillow in case she moved to the couch.

"Feeling a little better, thanks." She smiled at him. No need to drag Joel into her maudlin mope.

"Hey boy." Joel walked over and knelt to scratch Louie's ears. The dog closed his eyes and groaned in pleasure. "I always wanted a big dog." He twisted around to see Mara as he spoke. "I move too much and always live in apartments."

Mara's breath caught. His life seemed too lonely. "Why?"

"Why what?"

Why are you alone? "Why didn't you settle down?" This handsome man, animal lover, kid-friendly, and a Christian to boot. He had all the qualities any woman would look for in a solid, loving husband. So why wasn't he someone's husband? A little tickle started a meander through her thoughts. What kind of a woman would he want?

"I did. Remember I told you about Sherice." He gave Louie a final rub and moved to the sofa. "I was married for five years."

"I didn't realize it was that long. I guess I thought it was, I don't know, a short time." A crazy woman walked away from a generous, thoughtful, real . . . She really needed to stop making lists of his attributes or she'd be mooning over him after he left.

"Sometimes we don't have a choice in what happens. When we married, neither of us realized how circumstances would

176

change." Joel gave a small shrug. "She decided she wanted children more than she wanted me."

"What about adoption?" Sherice left a loving husband. "Couldn't you adopt?"

"Yes, but she felt strongly about having the experience of pregnancy." A sadness shadowed his being like clouds over a winter moon. "She had the right to make that choice."

"It didn't make it right though." Mara's voice took on an edge.

"People have free will and none of us make the right choice every time. I think back on those days. I was so caught up in chasing money, chasing success, and chasing the Fortune 500. I didn't understand how precious life and love were until testicular cancer took it away."

Mara felt the floor fall out from under her. "She left you with cancer?"

"No, she went through it with me. It was after I'd recovered. After all our efforts to have children failed."

"Even with all the scientific breakthroughs?"

"We tried before the surgery, but my count was already too low. My doctor suggested a fertility specialist." He pushed out a heavy sigh. "We tried it all. God had a different plan for me than I did."

"Joel, I am so sorry. The joy my children give me must be painful for you."

"Actually, I've really enjoyed your kids." He gave Louie a final scratch and then joined her on the sofa. "I was thirty when we married because I wanted all my plans set in place. I had to have money in the bank, a house, and car of my dreams. Don't laugh, but I even knew how many and when each child would enter our family."

She didn't laugh. Mara remembered the promise of her young married dreams. The way she and David would whisper on their pillows all the things they'd have and do together. So many left hanging like old spider webs in the basement. This man she first distrusted with every fiber in her body just confessed to pain as deep as her own. The pain may come in a different version, but this was not a mere gnat to be swatted away. He knew soul-searing, unfathomable pain equal to the loss of both her husband and her health. "I had no idea."

"I don't share that normally, Mara." He shivered. He seemed to release the vapors of lost dreams and then leaned back into the cushions. "I hope I didn't burden you."

"Not at all. In fact, I think you helped me get to know you better. Thank you for sharing. I'll tell you a secret."

"What's that?"

"I always wanted more kids. But with the business, I couldn't stay home with them."

"Would you still, if you could?"

She thought for a moment. "You know, if I had the time, I think I'd adopt a child."

"What makes you say that?"

Did she hear excitement in his voice? "After the Haiti earthquake, I realized how many children would need homes. But I haven't been in a position to offer the kind of attention a child would need, especially without a husband and the long hours I work now."

"But what if you had a husband? You could marry again." He gave her an encouraging smile. "I've often wondered if God would still give me the opportunity."

She took a long minute to answer as she studied his face. "You'd make a good dad. But I don't think anyone wants a lame, heart patient for a wife."

Where she once held a secret hope, the potential to love again, she now knew it would be next to impossible. Any man who might have been interested in a mother with three teens would run screaming from one who also had so many health problems. No more. Mara refused to think about wishes for nonsense. She'd be fine. She had three healthy kids and a company to run. Many women were not as blessed.

"I like to support homes for orphans now. It seems like some people are blessed with finances. So at least I can change lives that way." Enough of latent wishes, they didn't come true. Life wasn't about wishes. Mara pointed to the bell on the coffee table nearer to Joel. "How about a cocoa or something to warm you up?"

"Yeah," he smiled. "I could use one after the gusts out there." He rang the bell.

Cadence appeared, asked their order, and reappeared shortly with a silver tray and mugs of cocoa. She made a special show of adding toast triangles and mini marshmallows.

"I'm getting too used to home-cooked meals and the treats." Joel winked at Cadence who added her natural humorous flair to a bow before she retraced her steps to the kitchen to finish dinner.

"You know, I think the kids really like Mrs. Calder's kitchen lessons. My mom and Mrs. Calder have been splitting meal duty. When Mrs. Calder isn't cooking, my mom is organizing the kitchen to make it easier for me." She sipped her cocoa. "She thinks I relied too much on the Schwann's man.

He's on my speed dial."

She laughed. "Oh, I shouldn't be doing too much of that. It still hurts a lot to laugh." Mara pressed a hand over her stitches. "Whew. Okay, I do believe it's more important to sit down with my kids than to worry whether every meal is handcrafted."

"I think you're right and it's obvious how important it is because I can see the time you spend with your kids works."

Mara smiled at his compliment. She hated to do it to him again, but he deserved to be aware. "I need to let you know something about tonight's dinner."

Louie shook his head hard and bonked his nose on the floor. His sneeze came next in triplicate.

"Is he doing okay?" Joel asked.

"He seems to be slowing down more."

"Maybe you should have him checked out. He doesn't seem himself lately, at least not the guard dog I met last month."

"He's just showing his age and he misses David." Mara watched Louie again. "Like me." He could not pick now. She needed his warm doggy friendship, his faithful presence, and the last link to David. She couldn't take one more thing past what she dealt with already. She shivered. Then packed that worry down hard for another day. Definitely not today. She closed her eyes. "Tonight is —"

"Dinner!" Marisa called from the barbecue grill on the back terrace. David long ago hired an HVAC guy to install gas piping. They still grilled all year round.

Mara called back, "We'll be just a minute more." This would not be a fair situation if Joel walked into dinner blind. "Joel tonight is our anniversary, David's and mine." She dared a glance into his face. No irritation or resentment. He had the pure expression of one at a funeral. Sad acceptance.

"You still celebrate it?"

"The kids, well, you know." Awkward. She should have warned him the night of David's birthday dinner that this date was so close to the other. But until this moment, she hadn't felt the need. It hadn't mattered to anyone else beyond her little family nucleus. Who knew Joel would still be around? "It's so close to David's birthday. Once you start one thing . . ."

He nodded as he leaned forward. "I guess. No, I mean, yes, I understand completely." He sounded almost crushed and folded his hands between his knees. He sat quietly for a few minutes and stared at the wood flooring.

Was there more to his feelings? Or maybe

he was tired. He must be exhausted keeping up with her business and working each night with her too.

Would David always rule the house *in abstentia,* or would there ever be a chance for Mara and the kids to . . . To what? Joel rubbed the back of his neck. *What, Joel? What exactly do you want from them?* He needed to get his mind off ridiculous daydreams of having a family and tell Mara about the changes he'd made to her staffing. But she seemed so sad, so vulnerable tonight. The way she focused behind him on the wall pictures, dismissed Louie's condition, and sat a little hunched. Her normal uncommonly straight posture gave her a ballerina's elegance. "Are you in a lot of pain?"

"No, only when I laugh or sneeze. They have me on a good care routine. Why?"

Oh, good going, Joel. "You seem, well, off. Not yourself." He squinted as he watched her face. He'd wait on changes. She was not ready to deal with any of it right now. It might be a better idea to leave them to the celebration and slip out for the night.

As Mara talked about adoption, hope ballooned up inside him. Finding a woman who felt the way he felt toward orphans?

What were the odds? Obviously too high. This would be the first dinner he'd missed with them since he came a month ago. Joel stood. "You know, maybe tonight should be about you guys. I'll just run and grab a burger and we can start again tomorrow."

"Hey, Superman, you can't leave. I made you the biggest steak." Marisa stood in the archway to the dining room. "Grandma made all sorts of great stuff, too."

"Hon, I'm tired. So's your mom." He gestured at Mara in the recliner. "You've got a special dinner planned for her to remember your dad and I think she needs it."

Mara caught his hand. "I wish you'd stay."

Marisa's face showed the disappointment Joel felt.

His skin felt alive where Mara touched him. There had to be more to their relationship than imaginings loping around his skull. The catch was whether Mara felt it or not.

He shook his head. "No, Mara, I don't think so tonight."

The emptiness of two chairs at the table struck Mara hard. Her mother and all three kids passed the food around the table. Only the sounds of T-bones as they hit stoneware and the metal spoon as it scraped the vegetable dish broke the silence.

"Toby, would you say prayer please?"

They all bowed their heads. "Dear Big Guy . . ."

Mara blinked in surprise, but as she glanced around, the kids and her mom stayed in prayer. None of them flinched at the creative start to grace.

". . . Thank you for bringing Mom home safe so we can celebrate her anniversary with Dad. Please watch after Joel as he's not with us right now. Thank you for all the help he's done for us the last few weeks. Oh, and thanks for the food. Amen."

"Big Guy?" Mara asked.

Marisa giggled. "Yep, that's our new name for God."

"Uh-huh." She gave Marisa an indulgent smile. "Where'd that come from?"

Toby answered, "Joel."

Tonight the typical monosyllabic teen talk wore on her nerves. "A little more?"

Her mother explained, "He prayed with the children every day when you were in the hospital. It was heartwarming. He sure kept the family going, honey."

Marisa popped a green bean into her mouth and talked through her chewing. "He said God was a lot bigger than us and it helps him to remember that by calling him Big Guy."

"Makes sense." Joel certainly was a good influence for her family. A man who would lead her children in prayer? David was a good man who would appreciate the example Joel set for the kids. The loneliness struck her soul. But Joel needed a healthy woman, one who wanted a full home of children with him. Not one married to her work. Her salty steak tasted delicious but didn't quite hold enough appeal. Mara set her fork down.

"It feels weird without Joel here," Marisa said. Her fork bounced off the steak and not many beans disappeared. Odd, as the olive oil and balsamic green beans were Marisa's favorite next to Fry Bread at the fair. "He's been here every night." The fork began a faster rhythm as if she would tenderize the meat.

Cadence reached over and snatched the fork. "Seriously, you gotta stop doing that. You do it every time you —"

"Give her fork back please, Cadence."

"Only if she stops."

"Cadence." Mara lowered her voice. "I'm not up for this tonight."

All three kids turned and looked at her. No one said a thing as her statement sank

186

into them.

"Sorry, Mom." She gave the fork back with a glare at her little sister.

Marisa ignored her older sister's glare. "He's coming back, isn't he?"

13

Mara breathed in and saw her chest expand in the mirror. She could expand her lungs for the most part without pain from her ribs. She didn't feel like a hot poker shot through her either when she coughed. Over two weeks out and the surgery's success left her a long, thin wound she checked daily as her doctor instructed. But to her surprise, the scabbing looked worse than the healing scar. The thin line might not be as noticeable as she first assumed.

She was alive and would see Cadence's graduation. "Thank you, God." She found she meant it. The heart attack nearly created three orphans. Mara thanked God again. Who in the world would think a young woman at thirty-nine could die from a heart attack? Certainly not the doctor a few weeks ago that misdiagnosed her first heart attack as stress! She wanted to tell her friends to learn about their hearts. But she'd cut them out of her life like the surgery cut her body to repair the valve. Had she scarred her friendships beyond repair?

Mara frowned. She didn't really have women friends any more and her mother flew home yesterday. The house felt strangely empty without her puttering around and the kids all at school.

She could at least educate the women at work with a Wear Red Day and begin a Go Red for Women awareness. A wave of sadness washed over her. Friends. What had she done? She couldn't think of one woman she had spent time with in the last three years except for Mrs. Calder. She was truly a beautiful friend, but Mara recognized how closed she'd been to her church, Bible study, and anyone who knew the "before" Mara. All the platitudes and Bible verses pushed her over the edge and out the church doors. But maybe she'd been the one who pushed them away.

"Lord, please restore my friendships. I've really neglected them. I didn't even know I missed my friends." Mara wiped her damp cheeks. She missed the closeness of God, too. She'd replaced him with the idol of David's memory. "I've been so wrong. I do need you and the people you put in my life. I'm sorry." She paused and remembered the new name for God Toby had used. "I'm sorry, Big Guy."

The doorbell rang. She tried to hurry down the long hall with her contraption wheeling ahead of her. Louie already had his bark on.

"Mara?" The women's ministry director, Lisa Beecham, opened the door and peeked down at the dog. She held the door partially closed to keep the dog back.

"It's okay, he's happy to see you," Mara said as she wheeled across the last half of the living room. "Please come in." Mara pulled her thick sweater tighter against the frigidity of January and retied the belt.

"I won't bother you long. The ladies put together several meals after we saw your family last Sunday and I'm delivering them. May I?" She carried in two large grocery bags and set them down for a moment on the floor. Both were doubled for strength.

"That's so nice. Thank you."

"There's an envelope with a color-coded card with heating instructions for each dish. If you flip the card over, the recipe is written on the back so when you feel better, you can make your favorites. All the kids will need to do is read the card and follow simple directions." Lisa pointed, "Through there?"

"I'll show you." She led the way through the dining room. "My doctor says I have to walk a lot now in recovery. I was just getting dressed to go do that when you arrived. So, perfect timing."

Lisa picked up the bags and followed Mara into the kitchen. "It's sure a gorgeous, happy place in here." She pointed at the light lemon yellow sponge painting around the walls. "It's like a sunrise. Like a place brimming with hope."

"Thanks. That's pretty much what I was going for when I did it. The little bit of pink and peach with the yellow makes me think of the sun coming up over the Bridgers. Look, you can see them out the window over the sink." She leaned against the blush-colored quartz countertop. "Since I have to get up so early for work, I needed my kitchen to be a place I wanted to be in the morning." She looked around appreciating anew the room she'd designed and painted herself. "I wish I could be in here a little more."

"I know what you mean. It's just beautiful." Lisa began unpacking the bags and then created order out of chaos in Mara's freezer. "Mara, is there anything else we can do for you?"

"No, I'm overwhelmed by everyone's

generosity already." She didn't deserve such kindness after the way she'd ignored them.

Lisa turned around to face Mara. "Seriously. The last few Bible studies, many of the ladies have expressed a desire to do more for you. Several have jobs because of you. They want to make your recovery as easy as possible."

"I wish I knew what to ask for." What do you say to people who show love like that? People who didn't hold grudges against intentional neglect? *You were listening, God. But now I don't know what to do with your answer.*

"Are there any chores or things that you aren't able to do right now?"

Mara thought for a few moments while Lisa continued filling her freezer. Mrs. Calder came over each day and helped the kids keep up with the house. She was like family. They'd created a symbiotic relationship of give and take. Toby never had to be told anymore to shovel the walk for his adopted grandma. Outside of this unspoken agreement, she'd never asked for help before.

A nudge bumped against her conscience. She needed the memory quilt done. This could be the answer to her prayers. If she didn't accept now, she would never change.

It was time to let people back into her life. "Well, do you think anyone would like to help me with some quilting? I won't be able to lift the weight of the memory quilt I'm making for Cadence and I'll need someone to help me set up the rack." *There God, I did it. More? You want me to ask for more?*

"I'd sewn a few small sections together before my heart attack. I need to pin it up to sew into longer sections before bringing the face into one piece. Then I still have the batting, the backing, the edges . . ." Mara stopped her string of words. "I'm sorry. That's too much."

Lisa reached out and touched her shoulder. "I think we can arrange something. Several ladies at church either know how to quilt or have been learning."

"That would be wonderful." Lighter. Mara's spirit lifted like the mists that formed the clouds off the mountain foothills. Until that moment, she hadn't realized the depth of isolation she'd imposed on herself.

"Would it be too much to have two or three of us come at once? Maybe next week we could all sit down and have an old-fashioned quilting bee?"

A light bulb went off. *Yes. Yes,* she responded to the Lord's answer. "I think I'd be ready for a few hours of company by then." She grinned with a joy that glowed from deep inside. "I'll keep working on the embroidery and beading."

"Beading? Goodness this sounds like a complicated project. May I see it?"

"Absolutely." Mara led the way to the sofa. She lifted a pile of quilt blocks from the side table. "I've done more by hand than I expected because of my leg. I can't use the sewing machine as well with this cast on. The irony is they want me walking as soon as I can."

"You're getting around really well with the walking cast."

They sat on the sofa. It took a few minutes for Mara, but she managed to settle with the quilt blocks and her notebook. "Let's just say it took me twice as long to do the four laps around the hospital hall than the seventy-year-old who had surgery the same day."

Lisa rewarded Mara with a sincere laugh. "I'll bet that was a blow to your pride."

"Trust me," Mara wrinkled her nose, "I'm finding out my pride is a pretty silly thing to hang onto. At least I had the walking cast before the heart surgery." Mara rapped her knuckles against the fiberglass.

"I can't imagine." Lisa touched Mara's

hand. "How much longer for the ankle?"

"About another week or two." Mara wiggled the walker. "Have you ever seen a bigger basket case? I even have my own basket that hooks on the front."

Lisa laughed with her. "Mara, we've missed you. You are so loved and mean so much to the women of our church that we want to give back a tiny bit of what you've given us."

She'd given them nothing but a hard heart. Mara teared up. "I owe you all an apology." She swallowed.

"For what?"

"For avoiding and neglecting my friends. I've been angry from losing David. I'm so sorry."

Lisa hugged Mara with a tender embrace. "We love you and so does Jesus. We're all excited for the chance to show you that love." She sat back, relaxed. "So what about that project?"

Mara smiled and opened the sketchbook. "Here's what the quilt will look like through each stage." As Lisa oohed and ahhed over the pages, Mara lifted a few lines of hand-sewn pattern pieces of royal blue, forest green, and a deep red. "The stained glass effect happens with these tiny black pieces between each larger piece and around the arched windows. My favorite is the new champagne piping. It's from a special dress Cadence will wear in a couple of weeks."

"How will you use it?"

She'd thought of nothing else the last few days in the hospital. It helped her stay focused on recovery to have a creative plan alongside her complicated medical recovery plan. "To create the ribbon strand the dove's beaks hold. It'll weave through the entire border around the outside edge of the quilt. Then I matched embroidery thread to it for several of the window captions to carry the color." Mara flipped to the final drawing.

"That is the most stunning thing I've ever seen. Oh, I'm drooling over the chance to help you with this gorgeous present. Cadence will love, love, love this!"

They agreed on the following Saturday for a quilting bee. Mara's home would buzz with friendly voices soon.

Cadence ran in the front door. She dumped her books and slung her coat over the coat rack. She hugged Mara. "How you feeling?"

"Good, honey, still a little rough around the edges, but good." Since the surgery, Mara gave up secrecy. She couldn't move fast enough to hide her work and couldn't tuck something behind without pulling her body in directions it didn't want to go right now without serious complaint. She held up the block with Cadence in her powwow finery. The embroidery read, "Powwow Princess."

"Man, I remember that. I think I was like six or something." Cadence lifted the dangling needle on a long line of thread. "Did you just finish it before I came in?"

"Actually, I'm getting ready to do the special beading."

"What?"

"I'm going to put a few highlight beads on your dress and make it pop visually. It'll be traditional style."

"Oh cool! Mom, that's really cool. Can I help do the embroidery and beading?"

"No, Cadence, this is my gift to you."

"Mom, don't you understand you *are* giving me the gift. You're passing on the heritage and arts to me," she leaned forward as she spoke, "and now I want to learn it. I'm sorry I didn't want to learn before, I was just mad. But I do now."

Mara didn't know what to say. Would Cadence stomp off at the next wrong word again?

"Your mom taught you. Please teach me, Mom."

Mara thought for a moment about the discharge orders that dependence on others would be important to her full recovery. She battled against her desire to do it all herself when she invited the ladies. But didn't Cadence deserve the blessing too? The close relationship she had with her mother and grandmother came from the time they spent patiently teaching her this handiwork. They'd both made sure she would have traditions like this to remember. In the last few years Mara hadn't put any effort into passing on the beauty of her artistic heritage. A small step, but she wanted to change. Relationships had to take priority over her old habits.

She patted the couch cushion to her left. "Sit on this side." Mara pulled her sewing kit onto her lap and showed Cadence the right needles for beading. "These aren't the elk teeth beads because they're too big for this project. I picked the color to match the photo. My plan is to randomly attach some for effect. That way not all of them are covered. I thought if we picked a few small spots on various quilt blocks, the beading could pop dimensionally out of the photo. It'd be a similar idea to black-and-white photography where only one item is red against the degrees of black and white."

"It might look really cool. Then the design shape in the photo will stand out more. The elk teeth beads are too small in the picture to tell what they are anyway." Cadence looked closely at the quilt block. "What if we did the belt or boots instead? There's a lot of color and the lines are distinct. The beading would become the boots or belt."

Mara looked at the photo on the poplin again. Cadence had a good eye for design. "You know, I think you're right. But we need the tiniest needle to protect the transfer ink." After she picked out a thread to match the color, Mara showed Cadence the beading stitch. "Run the thread through a long line of beads like this. Then every third bead we put a tiny stitch. It'll keep the design meticulous."

"Tell me about when you learned this stuff."

Mara's father was already gone. With him went her link to her Irish roots. Her Crow grandparents, too. Her mother lived half the time in Arizona. Who would have told her children the stories had the heart attack been fatal? Who could have shared the art of the Crow women? Where would her kids learn of their Irish roots? *God, thank you for this second chance to do the things I'd pushed aside.*

14

Mara called Jill, ready to set up a part-time work schedule. Three weeks down and the doctor released her to light duty. He'd called her a model patient for following orders to complete detail.

"Constance Johnston, May I help you?"

"Excuse me?" Was there a temp for some reason? Mara worried Jill was out sick. "Who are you?"

"I'm the CFO of Bridger Pack and Rescue. May I help you, ma'am?"

"Oh r-e-a-l-l-y. Since when is there a CFO?"

"A few weeks ago." Though the woman's voice stayed polite, she took on a firm tone. "How may I help you?"

"You can't. I'll call back, thank you." Mara hung up. What was going on? In whose realm of being was any of this acceptable? A new employee for one of the skilled positions? She could understand if someone hadn't worked out Joel would need to fill it in quickly. But this, this mutiny would not happen! Mara punched the contacts list on her iPhone. Joel had another think coming if he thought he'd get away with hiring secret . . .

The doorbell rang. Mara glanced at the clock on the wall. No time to call Joel until after the quilting bee. She set the cell down on her end table. She sucked in deep breaths as Toby ran down the hall.

"Got it, Mom." He grinned at her. Toby held the door open for the ladies. Five women dodged Louie as they brought in armloads of food and sewing notions. Mara's mood lifted from the dull routine as she watched Toby's face. Both teen and dog nearly drooled while platters of food pranced by on the way to the kitchen.

Louie sat beside Toby like a footman. His head swiveled to follow each treat dance before his eyes.

"Such a gentleman."

"Truly polite."

Each lady dropped a compliment for Toby and a few patted the dog, too. Toby stood taller and then even offered his arm to Mrs. Calder as she came last up the walkway.

"You must be so proud of your son, Mara," Lisa praised as she watched him help their neighbor. "He's so much like his handsome daddy. I remember when David organized the car repair weekends for single moms. I see Toby turning into a man like that. Is it okay to tell you that kind of thing or does it hurt to think about David still?"

A soft spot warmed in her heart. "It's very all right, Lisa. Thank you." Mara took another long look at her son as he walked back in the door. Though his dark brown hair matched hers and hung to his shoulders, he had his father's athletic build and square chin. David's efforts to teach his son about masculine behavior paid off. Could he see this boy-man from heaven? She remembered many times David caught Toby's shoulder and drew him backward to hold a door for a lady in a restaurant or store. Gone three years and still his example lived on. A wave of gratitude washed over Mara for the focused attention from father to son. She hadn't met David until college, but he must have been much like the living legacy he left behind.

Lisa set her plate of chocolate chip cookies on the dining room table. "How's it going with Joel? Are you working from home?"

Mara pushed up from the couch. "Joel's been amazing."

At least I thought he was. She bit her

tongue so she wouldn't say that out loud. "He comes by every night and goes over the day with me."

She couldn't understand why he hadn't mentioned the new CFO. "We've set up a system to transfer files to my laptop. So I keep up as I can between physical therapy and follow-up appointments." She shook her head. "I feel like those appointments are a full-time job. But Jill and I are supposed to set up our schedule now for a few hours a day."

"You're amazing. I can't believe you aren't taking more time off."

"I did take a couple of weeks." Obviously three weeks too many, but she didn't want to share all the stress. "Joel worked some incredibly long hours keeping up with it all and his own job. The doctor's still not letting me do much yet. A lot of rest periods in the day after I walk, especially since I have to do PT for both my ankle and my heart. I'm just supposed to review the reports right now." *We'll see about that, doctor's orders or not!*

The other four ladies returned from the kitchen. Lisa introduced their newest member, Jenna.

"It's nice to meet you, Jenna, please make yourself at home."

"Pleased to meet you and thank you for letting us come and quilt with you." Jenna asked, "Would you like lunch first?"

Toby's ears heard that and answered before Mara had a chance. "Oh yeah, lunch! I'm starved."

And we're back to being a normal boy, Mara thought. If these ladies had any idea how much Toby and his friends could pack down in one night they might just run back out the door.

Louie turned and his back legs splayed out from under him. "Hey boy, that's some talent," Toby said. "Come on."

Louie didn't rise. His ears drooped and his tail flickered instead of thumped.

Toby knelt down. "What's up, dude? You need a lift?" Louie yelped as Toby picked him up in the middle and set him back on his feet.

Mara watched and wished she could help her old friend. "That's weird. He about did the splits. Poor old guy. Maybe the floor is too slippery with all the water."

Louie limped with stiff legs to the edge of the kitchen. He sat outside the arched door and licked his chops. "Yeah, Mom, maybe you should add a new hand signal if he can do that. Looks like he's okay though. You oughta have quilt ladies over every weekend,

Mom." Toby took off into the kitchen and scooted by the dog plopped down with his nose just over the stripping on the floor. "I'll grab the mop and then lunch!"

Mara grinned. Louie's habit of obedience, with a bit of personality, used to annoy David but always made her laugh. He pushed it sometimes like a toddler putting a toe over the line.

"Could you save some for us, Toby?" She called after her lanky son. The busy house added to her buoyant spirits. Maybe not every weekend, but it might be a good idea to be a little more social. Maybe she'd be recovered enough for the Museum Ball too.

Jenna touched her rounded tummy. "I'm looking forward to being a mom. I can't believe this little guy will be a man like Toby. It seems like waiting ten more weeks for him to be born is going to take forever."

"You found out it's a boy, huh?" Mara looked up at the infant portrait of Toby above the bookcase. Big brown eyes sparkled with humor even then. A lifetime ago. It felt like an entire lifetime had gone past in a flash. Where was the hopeful young mother with all the dreams?

Jenna nodded. "We figured some planning was a smart thing so we could budget."

Mara used her walker to meet Jenna in

the middle of the room. She had several sessions of muscle building to do for stamina and strength. "May I?" She held her hand near, but didn't touch the baby.

"Please do." Jenna stepped close enough for Mara to lay a hand on her tummy.

The baby rolled under Mara's hand. The two women shared a slow grin spread between them. "I think you're going to be a great mom."

"If I can be anything like you. I don't know how you do it."

Mara couldn't speak. Her eyes clouded with unshed tears. Jenna had no idea how difficult the last few years had been. Any mom could do a better job, be more available. Any mom who wasn't widowed, running a company, and trying to be both parents. What would it be like to go back to the days of being an expectant mommy before the company existed? Before she'd lost the love of her life? Before she'd exchanged her dream for the one she lived now?

"I'm sorry. You have such a hard situation. I didn't mean to make you sad."

Mara fought to regain control of her feelings. "Jenna, it's not you at all. If I could go back in time, I would figure out how to spend more time with my kids. I don't know how I'd do it. But I'd do it. These last few weeks you have, they'll fly by," she snapped her fingers, "and you'll wonder where they went. Then they're all grown up the next minute. I just have some things I'd do differently if I could."

Jenna touched her hand. "I think I'm going to pay attention to your wisdom. Thank you."

Mara smiled, "I hope you have the chance to build the family life you dream of, Jenna."

Lisa walked back in carrying two plates. "Here's a plate for each of you." She sat them on the coffee table.

"Boy, I'm thinking Toby is right and I should have you all over more often."

Jenna laughed. "I agree and so does baby here. Honestly, I didn't come for the food," she said as she prepared to bite into a finger sandwich. "I'm hoping to learn how to quilt from you. Nobody in my family ever did any sewing."

"Oh?"

"Lisa made me a beautiful layette set. I told her I wanted to learn how to do such beautiful sewing too. So when she said we could come to a quilting bee, I got pretty excited and here I am."

Mara's nerves frayed a little. "You have no sewing experience?" The same Spirit nudge that led her to invite the ladies kept her from saying more.

"Nope, not a bit."

"I, uh, I —" Cadence's quilt could be ruined if a complete newbie worked on the complicated pattern.

Jenna's smile slipped.

Lisa appeared and put an arm around Mara's shoulders. "Mara, do you think we could come up with some of the simpler things for Jenna to learn on?"

Simpler things? Mara took a minute to hobble over to the couch and sit. "I have some new paper designs for the border pattern. Would you be willing to help me cut out the paper and then use it to pencil trace on the back of the material? I can show you."

"I'd love that. But if I'm a burden to you, I'll just sit and watch. I don't want to cause you any stress at all."

Jenna's help in the final cutting would help. She had several small pieces left to do. "I tend to stand and lean over my work area when I'm cutting the fabric. It really would be nice to avoid some of that standing." Mara gestured at her leg. "I feel like I'm not doing as good a job as I could, but I get tired so easily. Don't you at this point, too?"

"You show the way and I will do as you

say. I heard this was the best part of pregnancy. I feel great. Always hungry, but great." Jenna finally took that bite. Then she dug into the rest of the food on her plate.

"Excellent."

Lunch finished, the ladies started clearing out the living room for the quilting bee. Mara showed the sketch of her design and gave the final instructions. Then she took Jenna and Lisa to her workroom. With Jenna and Lisa helping, they spread out the roll of paper Mara liked to use for her patterns. Jenna's steady hand used the paper stencil to draw the remaining border pieces. Satisfied with the care Jenna gave, Mara relaxed, chatted, and offered tips as she and Lisa cut out batting and backing. At this rate, most of the quilt top would be in position and many border rows stitched in place.

"Mara, I saw the beading and embroidery you've done on the quilt blocks. They're gorgeous."

"Thank you. Cadence actually helped on several. She wanted to learn our Crow tradition of beading."

"You taught Cadence while you've been home?"

"Yes, she took to it in no time. I think she has an artist's eye."

"I'm sure she does with you as her mom.

What would you think of teaching a class for church? Maybe we could use it as an outreach opportunity to the community."

"I can't do that."

"Mara, you're a good teacher. Look at how quickly you showed Jenna pattern cutting. You have her doing something she's never tried before and doing it well. You have more than a gift of design, you know how to communicate it to teach others."

Mara stopped her cutting. "I don't know. At this point, it's too much to think about."

Lisa nodded. "I agree it is, right now. Maybe it's supposed to simmer as an idea for a bit. I just thought of the potential. In fact, I think you'd be amazing at teaching anything to do with quilting, embroidery, and design too."

Jenna agreed, "I love the idea. I don't know what it'll be like to have a baby at home, but I'd be interested in learning. Maybe I could help somehow when you're ready, after I figure out this mommy gig."

Now Mara's head spun with the ideas. "Let me think about it." She didn't want to turn it down, but she also had an overcommitted life to get back into sync. But preserving the art of Crow beading, sharing the joy of creating art? It was a nice thought. A little flicker of fun flitted around her mind like a firefly. She tucked it away with other dreams that probably wouldn't ever happen.

Mara could hear the ladies in the living room laughing over stories of children and husbands. She drank in the sight of friendly faces working alongside her. Her home felt rich and warm with friendship. *Oh, God, thank you. Somehow, help me to find time for friends again.*

"So, are we going to meet this Joel we keep hearing about?" Lisa asked.

Then her mind turned again to the problem she had to solve next, the new CFO.

15

"Mom!" Toby yelled. "Mom, something's wrong with Louie!"

Mara grabbed her walker. "What's wrong?" She called back from her workroom as she completed the last border section on her sewing machine. "Did he stumble again?"

"Mom, you need to come here."

She moved toward the living room at a racing snail's pace. Another week and the walking cast would come off. It couldn't be soon enough. She edged closer to her goal feeling more like a peg-legged pirate. All she needed was a parrot on her shoulder. "Toby, what's wrong?"

Toby hunkered down beside the big dog splayed on his favorite pillow. Toby wore a grim expression. "He can't get up. He's tried, Mom, really tried."

She managed to get close enough to her son to lay a hand on his shoulder and not trip over the pillow edge. "He seems to be getting worse." She glanced at Toby. He swallowed hard and the deep brown in his eyes appeared glassy. "We need to get him to the vet."

"Cadence won't be home for another couple of hours. You want me to call her?"

"No, honey. She has to put in the time on her senior project. I'll call the vet and see if they can fit us in later this afternoon." Louie wagged his tail at her. He managed to pull himself up to his front legs with effort, but he couldn't get his back legs under him. He whimpered and fought to stay up. "Oh, boy."

Toby reached out to steady and calm his beloved friend. "I don't think we should wait, Mom. I'll call Joel." He started to stand, but then Louie tried to follow him.

"No, I'll call. I can't get down on the floor and love on Louie. You stay with Louie and help keep him relaxed."

Toby plopped back down beside the dog. He helped him get settled and stroked his head. "Good boy. There you go."

Marisa wandered into the living room as Mara dialed Joel. He answered after the first ring. "Hi. I'm sorry to bother you on your day off, but we kind of have an emergency. It's Louie."

213

"I'll be right over."

Mara opened the front door a few seconds later. "I don't know what to do. Louie can't go on pulling himself around by his front legs." She kept her voice low. "He's still wagging his tail. It's like he's so happy on the inside but the outside, I don't know, he's got so much spirit left."

Joel wrapped his arms around Mara. She leaned into him glad of his warm comfort. "Sometimes we have to just let go," he said. "His spirit is there, but his body isn't able anymore."

"I can't put him to sleep, Joel. I can't do that to him and the kids. He's all we have left."

Joel's face held such sweet compassion, "I know. But he's telling you he's ready. Maybe it's time to let go and move forward."

His words hit Mara off center. "What do you mean move forward, Joel? What in the world do you mean by that?" Mara's temper took over the worry. "Are you saying it's time to forget the past by putting Louie to sleep? I can't believe you'd say that to me!"

"No!" Marisa's eyes were wide with fear. "No, we can't forget Louie!"

At all the tension, Louie's ears flattened as if he'd been scolded.

"No, no. Please don't think I meant it that way. Marisa, Mara, I only meant to honor Louie's life by letting him move on. You'll never forget a dog as great as Louie." He shook his head. "Never."

Mara stifled her outrage. After the scare her children had had only a few weeks ago at potentially losing their mom, how could she even consider putting Louie down?

"Mara, can someone stay with him until he dies naturally?"

Mara blanched. She looked around at the depressed faces of her children. To sit on vigil and watch their dog die? With all they'd been through, they couldn't be asked to do it. "I guess not." She turned to gaze at her dog.

Louie raised his head at her attention and struggled again to get up.

"No, Louie." She said it as gently as she could. "Lie down. It's okay."

"Mom, no!" Marisa wailed. "You can't. You can't!"

"Marisa, we don't really have a choice anymore." Burning started in her sinuses as she fought for strength. "Honey, look at him. He's tired. I can't watch him suffer any more. That's not fair to him and honestly, I don't think any of us could take it either."

Marisa fell apart and wept. Joel touched Mara's cheek and left her to help Marisa. "You know, I think this guy is one amazing pooch. Why don't you tell me your favorite memory?"

As Marisa sniffled out how Louie always jumped on her bed to wake her up, Mara tapped Toby on the shoulder. "Hon, could you grab an old blanket for him? We'll make him as comfortable as possible on the way. Okay?"

Toby nodded, his voice sounded raspy and tight. "Yeah, sure."

Mara saw Toby wipe his sweatshirt sleeve across his eyes as he lumbered to the hall closet.

She dialed Cadence's cell. "Sweetie, could you please get a ride over to the vet's office? We need to take Louie in and I'm not sure what the outcome will be." She heard a sob and then a hiccupped yes before the line went dead.

Dr. Andrews shook his head. "I'm afraid there's nothing we can do. His blood work shows enough information to tell me he has cancer."

The girls gasped.

"Without a lot more testing, I'd hazard a guess that his loss of balance and the weight loss are due to pituitary cancer. It's not going to be long no matter what you decide. He doesn't seem to be in pain, but he's not going to be able to manage his own bodily functions from here on out. This dog has had the nine lives cats are supposed to." He stroked Louie's head. "This one, good boy, this dog I will remember. You've really done your job well here, boy."

Mara trembled. She had to make this decision again only a short few years after David's doctor suggested turning off life support. "I can't do it. He found him you know."

Joel asked, "Found who?"

"David. He found David after the avalanche buried him up at Hidden Gully."

Dr. Andrews nodded. "I remember seeing the news story. That was quite something."

Joel waited with a quizzical expression.

Mara wanted to share how heroic this dog really was. Maybe she just wanted to stall another minute, see the spark of life in her dog for a few more minutes. Maybe he'd rally one more time like after he took on the buck or after the second time a car hit him. They were sure each was the last. But he rallied back stronger with a will to live past any Lassie or Benji story. She sat down in the exam room chair. "David and his friends always took Louie to the mountains with them. They let him run around and chase snowballs. But when they got ready to ride, they'd put him in the cab of the truck so he wouldn't chase the sleds up the mountain. He'd sit staring out the back window like a statue as they all practiced hill climbs."

"I'm glad to hear he didn't ride with them."

Everyone had a small, nervous laugh at the thought of Louie riding a snowmobile.

Joel moved over to the chair, too.

Mara went on with the story. "That day, Louie sat in the truck as usual. There were only three men out and they ignored the avalanche reports. They'd been hill climbing that particular peak up at Fairy Lake for a few years and never had a problem. But the wind the day before had been intense. Then a big snow dumped on top of crusty old snow. David chased up the gully with his machine. He made it to the top cornice and stopped to wave. He put his foot down on what he thought was a rock. He cracked off an avalanche that snaked through the snow. David tried to swim the avalanche but it happened too fast and took him down. When Ben saw what happened, he left Kurt searching and he rode back to the truck and let Louie out. He told me he knew if David had any chance at all, it would be because Louie would find his owner for them."

Mara stopped to appreciate the gravity of what she'd share next. The kids knew the basics, but they'd never heard it in such detail before. "Our dog raced across the mountain. He zigzagged for a while and then started digging with every ounce of his being. Ben and Kurt grabbed the emergency shovels and immediately went at it. The men dug as fast as they could. As they'd get more snow out of the way, Louie pushed further in digging harder until his paws bled. They had to watch they didn't hit him with their shovels because nothing would stop Louie. It helped the guys know David was still alive when they'd see Louie wag his tail."

Marisa cried softly into Louie's fur. Cadence stroked Marisa's hair but kept one hand on Louie too.

"As soon as they had a space deep enough to reach David, Louie charged into it. They yelled at him to get out, but he'd curled up into David's exposed side. He somehow seemed to know David had to be kept warm as he struggled to breathe. Then they could hear David calling out. He was alive. Ben said he was in so much pain, but he kept praising Louie and encouraging the guys.

The sled had landed on top of him and created an air pocket. Without Louie, no one could have found him in time," Mara's voice cracked, "to let us have the last few days."

Joel dropped his mouth open. "I don't know what to say, but wow."

"I know." She smiled as she stood. "I think a dog like that needs his story told. He's full of courage, intelligence, and devotion like I've never seen before. He's, he's . . ."

Marisa finished for her, "The Chuck Norris of dogs!"

Toby nodded, "Oh yeah!"

Cadence grinned up through red-rimmed eyes and smeared black mascara. "Yeah, the Chuck Norris of dogs."

Joel put his arm around Mara's shoulders. "It fits."

Dr. Andrews gave a small nod to Mara and with the kindest tone said, "Why don't you all say good-bye now."

Mara shook her head fast. She wasn't ready. "No. He'll rally. He always does." Louie thumped his tail. "See?"

"Mara, he can't walk anymore. He can't tell me who's boss," Joel offered. "I think Louie is telling you good-bye already. Don't you?"

Toby hugged Mara. "Mom, Joel's right. We gotta do this. We gotta be brave like he taught us when he found Dad. It's our turn now to show him we can be brave, too, and love him enough to let him go."

Mara sniffed hard. She couldn't stop her runny nose or her shaking shoulders as Toby talked. Her son was the voice of reason. One that sounded so much like David, so much like his strength. When did he grow up so much? She nodded against his neck and clasped Toby to her.

Cadence leaned over and kissed his furry head. "I love you, Louie. You're the best dog anyone could have." Louie rewarded her with a tail thump and a lick on her hand next to his muzzle.

Marisa threw her arms around the old dog as he lay on the veterinarian's floor. "I don't think I ever said thank you for finding Daddy the way you did." She lay down beside him. "I don't want you to go." He licked her salty cheek.

Toby released Mara and watched his sister for a minute. "Come on, dudette." He stroked Louie's back. "We can't make him stay. There's lots of stuff for him to do up there in doggie heaven." Toby helped his little sister sit up and pulled her into his lap as he sat in the nearby chair. She wrapped her arms around her brother and cried.

"My shirt sure is getting soaked today."

Toby patted Marisa's back.

Marisa sat up and saw the wet patch. "Sorry." She fell back against him.

Joel put a hand on Toby's shoulder. "That's what big brothers are for."

Toby turned his face upward to Joel. "Yeah." He brushed the back of his hand across his eyes.

Mara's throat ached at the beauty of her son comforting his sister. Joel's support of Toby's place in the family, his mentorship, added a surreal element. Joel's approval ushered Toby into manhood in a way that would make David proud. Couldn't God just freeze time?

She had to hold it together for her kids. She soaked in what she could, but she had to say good-bye too. Louie looked up at her and struggled to lift himself. She had to spare him the pain and quickly signaled him to lie down. Razor-sharp still, he obeyed and let out a small groan.

Cadence muffled her cry behind her knuckles as she knelt to hug him. "I'm going to miss you so much, boy." She rubbed his soft ear between her fingers then pressed her cheek against his.

The vet, Dr. Andrews, reentered the exam room he'd left them in as he collected necessities. "Can I pray with you all?"

"Okay. I guess this is it," Mara whispered and knelt down on the other side of Louie from Cadence and Dr. Andrews. As she ran her hand along Louie's lean back, she thought about all the antics through the years. The laundry room door he'd eaten when they'd left him home over a weekend stood out in her memory.

The Calders felt awful when they came to walk and feed Louie. He'd presented himself proudly in a hallway full of shredded wood. They'd said he should have been Houdini on stage taking a bow with his tuxedo colors. That had been his first emergency trip to the vet — to remove the splinters from his mouth. The hint of a smile imprinted on her heart. She'd added the photo of Louie and the broken door to the quilt. Mara and Cadence laughed at the memory at the time. Now it would hold a more intense significance for the rest of Cadence's life.

Mara accepted Dr. Andrews' offer of prayer as the kids and Joel all knelt in a circle and held hands around the beloved dog.

"Lord, we thank you for the opportunity to know and love this pet. He's quite a special animal. You've given this family and me the honor of being stewards of your creation as we cared for him through his lifetime. We just want to thank you for the beauty Louie added to our lives. We give him back to you now knowing that you've shown us your love through Louie and shown us how to love better for having had him in our lives. Thank you for the Chuck Norris of dogs. In Jesus' name, Amen."

They all shared a subdued laugh as Louie flickered his tail.

"Be sure to give David a big old wet kiss from us, Louie." Mara scratched behind a soft, warm ear. "We'll see you one day soon." She kissed his fuzzy head and inhaled the familiar sweet scent of his fur. And the tears coursed down her face as the vet tenderly helped Louie to sleep.

Dr. Andrews squeezed Mara's shoulder. "I'll take it from here."

16

Tuesday afternoon Toby met Mara and Cadence at the door as they arrived home from physical therapy.

"Gotta call Adele back." Cadence tossed her coat on the rack and raced to call her best friend.

"Thanks for helping me out this afternoon, honey." It would be nice to drive herself again soon. Now she knew what it felt like to be completely dependent for transportation.

"Yep," she called back as she disappeared into the house.

"Mom, Dr. Andrews' office called. They have Louie's ashes ready to be picked up."

"Really? That was pretty fast." She hopped up the step with the aid of one crutch. "It's weird not having Louie meet me at the door. I keep looking for him like I did your dad."

"Yeah, me too. Sometimes I still look for

Dad." He gave Mara a side-glance through a long shock of hair. "So I was thinkin' it would be cool to maybe take him up to where Dad had his accident." Toby wiped his hands down his jeans. "I think that'd be a good place to, you know, like honor a great dog."

Mara stopped unzipping her coat and turned to Toby. "Up on the mountain? I don't know."

Joel arrived a few seconds behind Mara. He came up the walkway carrying two pizza boxes and a plastic bag of soda bottles. "Mrs. Calder's night off. I heard McKenzie River has the best pizza."

"That's right." Mara smiled at him. "Thanks."

"Hey, Toby." Joel looked between mother and son.

"Hey, Joel."

"Is it against the law or something, Mom?" Toby asked.

Mara took her time getting out of her winter gear as Joel handed off the boxes to Toby. He wisely stayed silent. The last thing she needed right now was more male input. "I don't think so." The cast didn't seem so difficult to maneuver any more, but she still had to sit to take off her one Ugg boot. She shuddered thinking of the avalanche. The bone-chilling cold that buried David.

"Mom, what do you think?"

"Can we all talk about it while we eat?" Mara pulled a sock off her cast soaked from the melting snow. "Get your sisters and we'll see." She wiggled cold toes. Three more days and the cast would be history.

"M'kay." He trudged off to the girls' bedroom doors. She heard him all the way down the hall and into the dining room. "Dudettes, dinner!" Then the pounding started. "C'mon, I'm starving."

Mara gave a small shake of her head. "I'm sure that's what I meant. Aren't you?"

Joel laughed. "Absolutely."

Together they set the table with the paper plates and plasticware.

Joel opened a cupboard and counted out five glasses. "What was he asking?"

"About spreading Louie's ashes up where David died."

Joel pulled packets of red pepper and Parmesan out of a little white bag. "Any problem with that for you?" He waited with the condiments in hand for her to answer.

Mara held a stack of paper napkins, "I didn't think I'd ever need to go there. It's where the whole world changed for me, for us." She tossed a napkin onto the plate in front of her with more gusto than it needed.

"I didn't think the kids would want to either."

Toby slipped into his chair. "I do, Mom."

"We do, too," Cadence added as the girls slid in behind Toby at the table.

Mara sat down as Joel opened the McKenzie River box. The delicious smell of chicken, artichoke, and cheese wafted across to make her stomach grumble. "Mm, smells so good." She tried to change the subject. "You're going to love this pizza. It's a Montana specialty. The company originated here."

Joel smiled at her and served up a piece to everyone. "Can't wait to try it. What do you guys say we pray over dinner and this decision you have to make?"

Marisa asked, "Will you pray? I like how you pray."

At Mara's nod, Joel offered prayer. "Dear Big Guy, we thank you for the food you provide. We thank you for the love you help us share. Tonight we ask you to guide this family as they decide how to best handle the ashes of their pet and the memory of their dad."

Marisa finished as had become her habit. "Amen."

They dug into the pizza and breadsticks. Cadence poured soda all around. "So, I kind of like the idea, Mom." She waited for the fizz to go down and topped off the glasses. "Toby told us."

"Me too," Marisa agreed.

Going up to the accident location held no appeal to Mara. Driving up on icy roads and trying to get across the snow with her cast were enough of a problem. But to face the place that stole David? "Kids, think about my cast. It's not going to work."

"Don't you get it off in a couple of days? We can wait 'til then."

"Please, Mom," Marisa begged. "I'll help you."

"I will too," Toby offered. "We can take snowmobiles in. You won't have to walk."

"Snowmobiles! You know how I feel about those machines." *God, is this what you really want from me? To take my kids to a place of grief on machines of death?*

Toby hung his head. "Yeah, I know."

Joel reached out for Mara's hand. "What if by going there and scattering Louie's ashes, you all found some sort of healing? Maybe it could become a place of remembrance instead of a place you fear."

Mara pulled away from Joel. "Taking snowmobiles into an area where we lost David isn't my idea of remembering. It's crazy!" The earnest pleading in the faces of

229

her children broke her. She bent over her food so they couldn't see the turmoil she felt. "I'm not going to talk about it right now."

"Maybe it's a way to help your kids say good-bye."

"Mom, come on," Marisa wheedled.

"We're not discussing it. The answer is no. Besides the fact I'll have a weak leg when my cast comes off, I'm also recovering from heart surgery in case you all forgot. I can't even think of how this might work."

Marisa piped up, "So ask the doctor."

Mara fumed. That was her best excuse and unfortunately, she knew the doctor would say what he said at her last appointment: Go until she was tired and then rest.

"Mom," Toby broke into her thoughts, "I just want to see where it happened. I want to see the place Louie saved Dad."

"Why? Why do you need to go there? Some things are better left alone."

"I want to go to the place Dad loved. I want to know why he loved it so much."

Cadence agreed. "I want to know, too. I've always wanted to put a cross and flowers where the accident happened, like they do on the highway."

"A memorial?" Mara hadn't thought of putting up a memorial before.

"That'd be really cool. We could find a spot to put the cross and maybe something for Louie too," Marisa added.

"Yeah, I like that idea." Toby nodded.

The idea of a memorial seemed too important for her family. "I'm not promising anything until I talk to my doctor."

"But you'll do it, if he says okay?"

Mara nodded. "If, and a big if, he says it's okay."

"Thanks, Mom. I promise you won't regret it," Toby said.

"Fine, fine." She swept a hand into the air. "But maybe we should have a plan B."

Cadence responded. "We can always think of another option. Seriously, we really want you to keep getting better. We love you, Mom." Her brother and sister chimed in and agreed. "Let's see what he says and maybe we could even take some chili and cocoa up like we did when we camped out with Dad.

"Man, I remember making a snow cave when Dad and I went ice fishing with Scouts and I earned a bunch of points toward my Hundred Degrees of Frost."

"Ha, I remember hearing your gear all went in the lake."

Joel laughed. "Your gear went in the lake?"

"Just my sleeping bag. All the guys

chipped in blankets and stuff while we hung it by the fire. Besides, one of the guys lit a Sterno can and the snow cave got so hot inside we were all sweating."

"Pretty ingenious, Toby."

"My dad showed us how to build it. He did all the survival stuff for our troop." He leaned across the table and took a bread-stick. "I miss doing that stuff, you know."

Joel took another piece of pizza. "The survival stuff?"

"Yeah, that and Scouts."

"I was an Eagle Scout. Maybe I could help you out."

"Yeah?"

"Sure, let me see what you have left to do."

"Cool."

Cadence pulled out her phone and punched the weather app. "Check it out you guys. We're supposed to have warmer weather the next few days. No blizzards and wind. It'll be fun!"

Mara nodded, but inside she knew the avalanche that took David swallowed her too. No promise of good weather would change the fact she didn't want to see that place. But her family did. Her children needed the closure she hadn't allowed because of her own anger. Wasn't being the parent left behind supposed to get better with the passage of time? Somebody forgot to make it easier. She looked heavenward with a sense of irreverence. "After I get the cast off Friday, okay? We can go on the weekend — if the doctor approves."

"Really?" Marisa squealed.

"Really." Now all she needed was for the weather to stay warm and melt off the roads. There'd be no excuses to back out. Somehow in her spirit, Mara felt God smile and knew the rest of the week would be Montana's winter version of balmy. *Great, I thought we were on the same side, Big Guy.*

"So why don't you gals let Toby and me clean up." Joel gave Toby a stern look he hoped communicated he wanted to talk privately.

Mara lifted her brows. "You want to clean up?"

"Well, since you're coming back to the office now I feel guilty that you're not getting as much work done on the quilt for Cadence."

Cadence looked up surprised. "You've been paying attention to my quilt?"

"Are you kidding? That's an amazing piece of art. I check it out every time I come."

Cadence smiled. "That's cool." She turned

to her mom, "So, want to go work on it with me?"

"Actually, yes, I do."

"I've got a science project I have to get done." Marisa screwed up her face. "No school on Friday, teacher in-service. So 'stead of letting us turn in our projects on Monday, we have to have them in on Thursday."

"Alrighty, boys, it's all yours." Mara pushed back from the table and limped her way down the hall with the girls.

"Dude, you put us on kitchen duty?"

"Toby, I have an idea and I wanted to see what you thought of it first."

"M'kay. What's up?"

Joel picked up the empty pizza box and loaded the used plates. "What do you think of using your snow cave skills again?"

"It's a blast, sure. When do you want to go?" Toby tossed the rest of the trash into the box.

Joel stepped over to the dining room arch and checked to see that the girls and Mara were not in hearing range. "I thought I'd take the day off on Friday and create a surprise for your mom and sisters, if you want to help out. We could head up to Fairy Lake area and build a snow cave."

"Whoa, cool . . ."

"You have anything happening that day?"

"No, but how are we gonna get it done in time without them all knowing? It's a couple hours round trip plus building the cave."

Joel thought for a minute. "How many guys you know that might want to help out?"

Toby laughed. "My whole troop. And, dude, a bunch of 'em have snowmobiles."

"Tell you what. You get whoever wants to come along and have them bring some gear. I'll set it up for us to get some time away and keep it a surprise." Joel stuck out his hand. "Deal?"

Toby grabbed it. "Deal, dude."

Saturday's sunshine warmed Mara's face through the windshield of the Jeep as she pulled her trailer with a double-seated snowmobile away from the rental company. She loved the sense of freedom. Her leg felt a little weak, but for the most part she relished sitting in the driver's seat again.

Toby entered the GPS coordinates for Fairy Lake into Mara's Garmin.

"Is that something you learned from Scouts?" Mara asked as she drove away from town up toward Bridger Canyon Drive. The high mountain lake, camp-ground, and recreation area sat in the Bridgers just below Sacagawea Peak.

"What?"

"You used specific degrees." She pointed at the GPS. "I've always used the name or address of a location." They didn't really need it today, but the small piece of equipment had saved Mara from the infamous are-we-there-yet questions over the years. Whoever sat shotgun also took charge of the GPS and answering any questions about location or distance.

"Oh." He looked out the window. "Um, I just thought it'd be cool to try it."

Mara tried to catch his attention as she looked at the road and back at him. Something struck her as awkward. "Are you avoiding me for some reason?"

"Nope. Just hangin'."

"Hmm, okay." Mara glanced in the rear-view mirror at her daughter's head bopping to music. "You good back there, Cadence?"

Cadence pulled out her iPod earbuds. "What?"

"You good?"

"Sure, Mom." She smiled. "I'm really good. It's going to be a great day." She replaced the earbuds.

Mara appreciated the positive attitudes, but she wasn't as convinced the day would turn out so well. Riding a snowmobile could be too rough even for a short ride. Worst-case scenario, she'd have to wait at the parking area while the others went in and set up the memorial. But first she'd try — for her kids.

Marisa rode with Joel in his SUV. They pulled another trailer with two sleds on it. Her youngest was so excited that Mara almost felt sorry for Joel. Almost. Marisa would chatter non-stop. She hoped Joel had a lot of patience for the drive, all the way up, until they unloaded for the day.

The blue sky, brilliant white snow on the mountains, and pleasant forecast would normally lift her attitude too. She loved to ski with her kids at Bridger Bowl. As a family they'd been on the slopes every winter — not as often since David died. But today the sunny skies and dry roads meant she had to make good on her promise and keep driving.

An hour later their mini-caravan parked at Toby's coordinates. Everyone worked together and they prepared for the short jaunt to the foothills. Mara carried the lighter items to stow in the saddlebags.

Cadence hopped on and fired up her solo machine. "Let's get this party started."

Toby reminded Mara of David as he climbed on the first double-seater. "Come on, dudette." Toby waved Marisa on the back.

She clambered on. "Let's go cowboy!"

Joel laughed at Marisa's excitement and sat on his snowmobile. "Mount up, Mara."

She looked all around the group. It seemed more like a fun winter outing than the planned memorial. "Okay, but we need to take it slow."

"Like a turtle."

His smile charmed her right down into her snow boots. Both of them. She balanced on her stronger leg and slipped on behind Joel.

"Remember we're stopping past the tree line to see how your mom is doing," Joel shouted over the engine noise.

"Mom?" Cadence called over to her. "You good to go?"

Mara tamped down her nerves and hoped the forced smile looked genuine through the helmet faceguard. She yelled back the same thing Cadence had said in the car. "I'm really good. It's going to be a great day."

Cadence gave her a thumbs-up.

The group started off away from the parking area. The back of the snowmobile vibrated more than Mara expected. She pressed her hand against her chest.

Joel looked over his shoulder and shouted over the engine, "Are you okay?"

"I think so." Her answer came out a bit breathy as she tried to yell into his ear.

"Lean into me and let me take the brunt of any bumps."

She paused for about two seconds. Then the snowmobile ran over a rough patch. Mara took him up on the offer and scooted closer to Joel. The stability of his back offered her more support. She braced more comfortably. His strong shoulders did help absorb the uneven jaunt.

The ride didn't last long. As they broke into the open, Mara's gaze drew upward to the highest mountain in the Bridgers, Sacagawea Peak. She gasped at the majestic scene. Pristine snow sparkled in the sunshine and rippled across the foothills like frozen waves depositing diamonds. David would have chased every gully between the swells hunting for his treasured adrenaline rush.

Mara whipped her head around at the sudden screech from Marisa. What was wrong? Her helmet settled off-kilter so she had to grab the bottom and twist it to see.

"Mom!" Cadence yelled. "Look!"

Mara followed the excited point from the tip of Cadence's heavy blue glove exactly opposite of where she'd been staring. A snow castle? How in the world?

"D-u-d-e!" Marisa jumped off her seat and ran over to them. "That is the most awesome thing I've ever seen!"

Joel helped Mara off the snowmobile. "Do you like it?"

"I —" Mara stood transfixed.

Cadence looked from Toby to Joel with a suspicious expression. "Wait a minute. Did you guys know this was here?"

Toby laughed at her. "Good sleuthing, Sherlock. We built it yesterday."

His sister rewarded him with a withering glare that lasted a split second. The castle's existence softened her response. "It's too cool, little bro." She yanked off a glove, pulled out her phone, and snapped a photo. "I think this will be a perfect thing to add to my senior project. What could be more 'made in Montana'?"

"A slide!" Marisa's voice went up an octave. "Man, an actual slide! C'mon, guys, we have to go try it out!"

The snow castle was massive with a turret on the second story, an ice slide that faced downhill off the top platform, and windows cut out of the sides. Set in the middle of the wide field, it could be something out of *The Lion, the Witch, and the Wardrobe*. Mara drank it all in. "I saw a small one like this on the news a few years back. Somewhere in Michigan, I think. A family built it over the winter. But this is — I don't have words."

"Are you up for an afternoon here?" Joel asked. "We have the perfect spot to set up our chili and cocoa."

"It's magical." She took in the mountains behind the castle where David's accident likely happened. *Oh, I don't want to be here.* But it didn't feel as oppressive as she feared. The pine trees rustled with a light breeze in the distance. The brilliant reflection from the snow and the vibrant blue above created an achingly beautiful scene. Without her shaded goggles, she couldn't have handled the intensity. "How did you manage to build something so magnificent in one day?"

Toby strode over and put an arm around her shoulders. "It was Joel's idea. We called in all the troop."

"Your Scout troop?" She stared at Toby. "How? When?"

Joel motioned to Cadence to come over. "Yesterday when I told you I had some personal things to attend to, well, this was it."

"I'm stunned." Mara sat down on the

thick padding of their snowmobile.

"But you like it, right?" Toby asked. "We had fifteen guys making snow bricks and building. Took all day."

"Who wouldn't! This is incredible."

"Can we check it out?" Marisa yanked on Toby's parka.

Joel took the lead. "Let's park these things right over by the castle and have some fun."

Fun. Not her expectation for today. What was wrong with fun? How long had it been since she'd really allowed herself to play? She grinned at all the kids, "Well, what are you waiting for?"

Once parked, they left all the helmets with the snowmobiles. Toby and Joel invited Mara to tour the castle.

"Your Highness, may I present to you the entry that leads to your banquet hall."

She laughed at Joel's feigned British character. "Amazing. I can't believe you guys built an actual table and chairs." Mara ran her mitten across the top of the ice table. The piled snow was pressed hard on top and leveled. Six chairs popped up like mushrooms from the floor in the tight space. A small staircase led up to the turret above with cutouts to see the mountains.

Toby shrugged as if building all the amenities was the most natural thing in the world to him. "We used a five-gallon bucket to scoop snow for the seats and most of the table. Jeff had a bunch of big Tupperware containers his mom let us use for making bricks."

"Toby, I can't believe how incredible this is."

Toby's chest puffed out at his mother's admiration. "We knew we needed a spot to eat lunch."

Mara laughed. "Then let's do it."

Marisa ran past them and up the stairs. "Not yet. I have to try the slide."

"Me too!" Cadence followed her sister.

"It's fast." Joel explained, "We decided to ice it with a layer of water before we headed home. We dumped what was left in the jugs we brought along for drinking water. Then the boys threw in a little creativity. They used some water to ice down the landing area too. You go down and you keep going for fifteen to twenty feet."

Mara laughed again. "It helps you have the slide pointed downhill."

"Well, we are rocket scientists," Joel teased.

"Oh, yeah. I'm so on it." Marisa swung into position just out of sight from Mara. "See ya on the flip-side." Down she went in a peal of laughter. She kept on sliding to the end of the ice, laughing so hard she couldn't get up. Everyone chased her up and then followed Marisa down the slide. Cadence and Toby slid right into her, all three toppling like bowling pins.

Mara went after Joel. They'd smoothed it of any bumps. She swept down the slope and slid to a stop in a fit of giggles.

Joel helped her to her feet. The kids already ran back into the castle for another slide challenge. He pulled her out of the way in time for Toby's backward arrival. He kept his arms around Mara and she didn't shake them off. A little bubble of joy pinged around inside her.

"Now you guys have to come down backward," Toby taunted his sisters.

"Hah, we'll one up you!" Marisa stuck a number one sign in the air. The girls sat down together and linked legs. They held their tandem position until they hit bottom then twirled out of control with hoots of laughter.

Mara smiled up at Joel. "Thank you. I can't think of a better way to honor their dad. If Louie were here, he'd be chasing the kids up and down the slide too."

Joel didn't break eye contact. Instead, he dipped his head down and kissed Mara's lips. Not a long kiss, just long enough to send a tingle through her blood. Long enough to awaken wonder. Then she realized the kids might have seen the kiss and panicked. She backed away as Cadence zoomed by their feet and rolled into the snow a few feet past them. Marisa kept rolling as far as she could push the momentum.

Joel didn't stop Mara from pulling away. Instead he directed his attention to Cadence. "I heard you say you have a senior project due next month." He reached out a gloved hand to help her up. "Something to do with photography?"

She latched on to his grip and vaulted up. "Yep, I'm creating a project that shows what life is like in Montana on PowerPoint and a small brochure. I'm working with a mentor from the Montana Office of Tourism to show family-friendly activities. If she likes it, they might actually use my project to create a commercial or something. But I have to turn in my progress on Monday. They're picking the top ten ideas to spotlight on the news!"

Mara knew Cadence was talking, but she couldn't hear a word she'd said. He'd kissed her. Joel planted one sweet kiss right on her very lonesome lips. And his kiss opened up a wash of emotions. Mara squinted hard against the brilliance of the day, the long drive, and the excitement. She needed a few minutes to pull her head together. "Hey, I'm going to let you guys keep going, but I think I need to go take a rest."

Both Joel and Cadence turned concerned faces toward her. Joel asked, "Do you need anything?"

"Nope. I'm just feeling a bit tired. Doctor's orders — I have to take a time-out. I'll try those fun little stools you all built in the banquet hall." Mara hoped her voice sounded natural to them as she turned to head up to the castle.

"I'll be up in just a minute," Joel said. "Cadence, could you do a picture for me of the family with the castle before we leave? I'd love to have a great one to remember you all by."

Mara suddenly stopped in her tracks. *To remember us by?* She looked back at the man who'd given her her first kiss in three years. Sure, it made her nervous, but he also tingled her blood right down to her toes. Of course, Joel has to leave. She realized how odd it must seem to stand there and started walking again. Then why would he start something he couldn't finish? Wait. *Who said anything started?* "God," she whispered in her heart, "what are you doing?"

■ ■ ■ ■

Joel watched Mara hesitate and look back at him as she walked uphill. He hadn't meant to kiss her right there in front of the kids. Had he pushed her too far? Today he wanted to help her family spread Louie's ashes, not stress Mara. But in all honesty, he'd been thinking about kissing her since the first day they met. Since he saw her snore in the brown recliner. A slow smile spread across his face at the adorable picture in his head. Yes, since then.

Marisa ran up. "Race you."

They all took off. The girls ran to the side of the ice field. Joel tried to cut them off by going across it. Joel laughed as he slipped and went down flat on his belly. The girls circled back to him and stood giggling over him. "Okay, so snow boots are not made for running."

Toby slid by them on his next daring dart down the slide. "Whoa, watch out!" He swished off to the right.

Joel's feet couldn't get traction and splayed out behind him. He managed to get up off the ice after several tries with the girls tugging on his hands.

Marisa held her stomach. "That was like

Bambi on the pond."

"Hey, I thought my nickname was Superman, not Bambi."

The girls doubled over and laughed at him.

Toby jogged up to them on the snow pack, avoiding the slide's ice patch. "Well, on your belly like that you're doing the Superman. Now you oughta do that goin' down the slide." He held his arms out in front. "But don't forget this."

"Yeah, yeah. You guys laugh." He grinned. "I was just making sure I had an empty stomach for lunch."

"Uh-huh." Cadence chuckled. "Sure you were."

"So how about that lunch?" Joel looked up toward the ice castle. Mara stood in the doorway. Her eyes crinkled with laugh lines as she wiped away tears. *God, I love her and I love these kids. So what do I do about that?*

Mara waved a hand. "Come on you gooses. Grab the packs, I'm starving."

Joel and the kids unloaded the packs and set up the table. Laden with paper cups for both chili and cocoa, they all sat down. "Tight quarters." Joel bumped shoulders with Toby and caused smiles all around.

"Yeah, but no wind. It's pretty cool in

here." Marisa laughed at her irony. "I mean warm."

After they offered grace, Mara filled paper cups with chili from a thermos. Cadence poured out the thermos of cocoa. The aroma of spicy chocolate steam filled the small space as they ate.

"Mom, how're we gonna, you know, take care of Louie's ashes?" Toby asked between bites.

"Well, I thought we could take the snow-mobiles up to the tree line below the area Kurt and Ben said the accident happened." She took a deep breath. "We have to be very careful. With the warm weather, I don't want to trigger or even come close to another avalanche. I think Daddy ended up lower anyway based on what they told me."

Marisa nodded. "I'm a little scared, too."

"Honey," Mara smoothed Marisa's cheek, "I like the idea of erring on the side of safety."

Toby rolled his lips inward, deep in thought. "What if we carved their names on a rock or in a tree?"

"Ooh, I like that idea." Cadence agreed. "It's not like we can build anything. People come out here to snowmobile and cross-country ski all the time."

Joel stayed silent, watching. This time, this

choice belonged to the Keegan family. Would they be able to release the pent-up grief?

Mara's expression looked wistful. "I like that, too. We can clean up here and then go look around. Okay?"

The cold mountain air seemed to make them all hungrier. The second thermos of chili passed around the table before they cleaned up.

"Okay, I've got a timer on my camera. We need a great shot of us with the snow castle for Joel to take home." Cadence stowed her share of the gear and pulled out her small camera case. "I think I could set up the camera on the seat here if you'll all get in place."

They obeyed and stood in a straight line in front of the castle.

"Oh, no way." Cadence shook her head with emphasis and crossed her arms. "That is the most boring pose I have ever seen! This picture could be famous. It could be on my brochure or on a commercial."

"What do you want us to do, honey?" Mara looked perplexed.

"Dude! I've got an idea," Toby announced. "Let's look like we're playing on the castle or something."

Joel tossed out an addition. "Great idea.

Toby, get up and sit on the slide. Marisa, you get behind him like you're waiting on your turn. I'll get some snowballs and pretend I'm going to toss them off the turret."

Mara laughed up at Joel. "What a fun idea. I can pretend I'm throwing snowballs back at you."

He held himself back from stealing another kiss. But the sound of her laughter did something to his insides. He warmed in her presence more than the entire thermos of cocoa could do.

"And I'll set the camera then jump in somewhere." Cadence went to work finding the right spot on the seat for the camera to balance. As soon as they had a pile of snowballs for both Mara and Joel, she adjusted each person's placement in the frame. "Mom, you need to go about a foot in toward the door. Okay, now Joel, lean down just a little so I don't cut your head off."

He lifted his foot up onto the top level of ice bricks and put one hand on his hip and an arm balanced across his thigh. Then he mimicked a magazine model looking off into the distance.

Marisa giggled at his *GQ* pose. "Off with his head!" she stated. "That sounds more like what the queen of the castle would say than someone taking a picture."

Cadence grinned up at them and called out, "Hang on, I'm taking a few and checking the lighting."

"This is going to be a fun memory," Joel said without breaking his pose. A whomp landed right on his chest. "What?" He looked down to see Mara winding up another pitch as everyone burst into laughter. "I thought you weren't supposed to do anything strenuous."

"Oh, that was an easy target."

He went for a snowball.

"Nope, I'm coming in. You kids settle down now." Cadence raced into her chosen spot at the bottom of the slide and threw her arms in the air. She looked like she had just come down the slide.

The camera flashed twice. Marisa gave a huge heave. "Hey, dudette!" Toby went flying down the slide. Cadence pushed off with her hands to stay ahead of Toby's feet. The camera flashed twice more.

"Let me see if we got one," Cadence called from the bottom of the ice field. She trudged uphill.

"Mara." She looked up. Joel tossed a handful of snow down. He caught her by surprise in the face. "That's what you get for messing with the king of the castle." He brushed off his hands.

She brushed off her face and laughed. "Yeah, I deserved that." And he wanted to kiss her more.

"Got it!" Cadence shouted in triumph. "Got a great one!"

"All right, load 'em up." Joel jumped over to the slide and launched himself down on his stomach, arms outstretched like Superman. He hurtled to the bottom and past the ice field to the kids' whoops and hollers.

"That was awesome!" Toby offered a high-five as Joel made it up the hill to the snowmobiles.

"Had to live up to my name." Joel met his glove in a muffled slap.

"You sure did, Joel," Mara whispered to him as he climbed on the machine. Was that admiration in her voice? Joel glanced back at her and was rewarded with a glowing smile.

They rode away from the snow castle near the trees on the other side of the clearing. Joel took the lead and followed north along the line to the first gulley. He drew to a stop. The others pulled up alongside. "Is this a good spot?"

"I like it. The spot David loved is right there," Mara said and pointed up at Sacagawea Peak. "What about you guys?"

Everyone agreed.

Toby took off his gloves and dug in his pack. Marisa jumped off the machine to give him space. "Whatch'ya doing?" she asked him.

"I've got my pocket knife in here. See that tree?" He tipped his head. "It looks like it's in a perfect line of sight right to the peak. I can carve it."

"I'll help you." Joel found his pocketknife too. "What if I do Louie's on the next tree over?"

They went to work. Joel knelt in front of the tree to carve. He didn't mind the girls directing him. After all, it was their dad and dog. "A little bigger, 'kay?" Marisa asked.

"Sure." He dug a little more bark loose. "Like that?"

"Yeah." She smiled.

"These trees are a bit too narrow for much more than the names," Joel suggested as he turned on his knee to check with his task-masters.

Mara offered, "I think their names are enough. We don't want to kill the trees anyway."

Cadence came forward with Louie's ashes. "Maybe we'll help the trees heal a little when we put Louie's ashes by them."

Joel nodded. "Pretty good plan."

Mara took her gloves off. "Do you all mind if we offer up a prayer?"

"That'd be cool." Toby stood back from his tree carving. *David Keegan* rolled around the trunk and Toby added *2010* below it.

Joel walked over to his saddlebag. "I have something else I'd like to offer." He put away his knife. He rummaged a little more and took out a small bag.

"What's that?" Mara asked.

"I made these last night in case we couldn't figure out something once we got up here." He handed the plastic bag to Mara.

"It's heavy. What's in here? Rocks?" She knelt down and unwrapped the grocery bag. Two smooth painted stones with Louie and David's names tumbled out onto the ground. She gasped. "Oh, Joel, that's so thoughtful. You've got the date and everything."

He hunkered down beside her as the kids followed suit. "I wanted to make sure you guys had what you needed."

Toby took the stone with David's name on it and placed it tenderly at the foot of the tree he'd carved while Marisa took Louie's and put it by the other tree.

Cadence wrapped her arms around her

little sister as Marisa dropped back into their circle on the ground.

"Thanks, Joel," Toby said in a thick voice.

"One more thing, if you don't mind. I found something in Isaiah I thought might fit the ceremony." He reached into his coat pocket and unfolded a piece of paper. "I wrote it down since I thought it might be a little rough to bring a big Bible." He read the note to them, "The LORD God's spirit is upon me, because the LORD has anointed me. He has sent me to bring good news to the poor, to bind up the brokenhearted, to proclaim release for captives, and liberation for prisoners, to proclaim the year of the LORD's favor and a day of vindication for our God, to comfort all who mourn, to provide for Zion's mourners, to give them a crown in place of ashes, oil of joy in place of mourning, a mantle of praise in place of discouragement. They will be called Oaks of Righteousness, planted by the LORD to glorify himself."

"That was beautiful, thank you." Mara's eyes shimmered. She bowed her head and started praying. "Lord, we've — I've felt brokenhearted and like a prisoner to my grief. I ask you to give me joy instead of mourning for my children's sakes. I ask you to help our family let go of our despair now

256

and be full of praise. Thank you for the life of David and the joy of our loyal dog, Louie." She looked up at everyone. "Anyone else want to add anything?"

"No, that was good, Mom," Cadence answered in a hoarse voice. "Okay with you guys if I sprinkle out the ashes now?"

Everyone nodded and stood together. Cadence walked to the trees and shook out the little box the vet provided. She sifted half at the base of one tree and half at the roots of the other. Then she came back to the group and hugged each one. They all hugged each other as well.

Joel's last hug came from Mara. As she leaned into him, he inhaled her sweet scent and said a silent prayer of his own. *Lord, I'd like to be this family's sturdy oak. Show me how if it's your will.*

Mara arrived at the office an hour before everyone else on her first Monday morning back to work. She looked around her office. Still clean and well-ordered, somehow the sparse desktop had a more masculine feel.

She dialed the phone. Mara delayed the talk with Joel for the dog, her cast removal, and the memorial. Now it was time to get back to work, and she couldn't, without knowing what was going on and who worked for her.

"Joel, we need to talk."

"I'll meet you at the office shortly." He answered over the phone. "I have a stop to make on the way."

Mara fumbled through the minimalist stack of paperwork in her inbox. A card from her employees she set up on her desk, a task hot-list from Jill, and the list of new employees from Joel. Perfect, Constance was on the list and exactly the issue she wanted to discuss with Joel. Why hadn't he told her he'd hired a CFO? He must have worked an unheard-of schedule handling his own coaching plus her office. She'd try to give him the benefit of the doubt.

She reviewed three or four new employee files and uploaded some new design photos to the Bridger Pack and Rescue website by the time he walked through the door. He held something behind his back.

"Morning, early bird." Joel brought a bunch of purple hybrid orchids mixed with lily of the valley. "To welcome you back."

"Oh." She stood up from behind her desk. "Thank you."

"I knew your favorite color, but I don't know your favorite flower." He offered a sheepish smile. "A grocery store is a bit limited this time of the morning."

"I don't really have a favorite." She cradled the flowers. "They're like God's art to me so I love them all." *I think I'm falling for you, too. Did you have to make it so hard to talk business?* She snuck a glance from under her eyelashes.

"Shall we get to work?" He pulled out a chair from the front of Mara's desk. "Your first day back at work. How's it feel?"

"Actually, I'm a bit concerned." Mara set the flowers in a coffee cup and leaned them against the computer monitor.

"Well, that's understandable." Joel nodded.

"No, I mean over some of the changes."

"Ah, gotcha." He sat forward on the chair. "Where do you want to start?"

She slid a file over to him. "How about with the new CFO?" Mara didn't take her eyes off Joel's as she measured his response. "Who authorized this?"

"Mara, somebody had to do payroll and taxes. What else was I going to do to protect you, I mean your company?"

"But this is something we should have talked about first."

Joel nodded. "I completely agree. But that was on our agenda when you ended up in the hospital a month ago."

The time frame stuck in her craw. "You've had a month to tell me?"

"Mara, I'm sorry for not telling you. I just felt like you needed the extra support. Then things kept happening. I couldn't tell you with Louie dying. It would have been unkind. Then there was so much stress." He ran a hand through his hair. "I'll be honest, I didn't want to tell you over the weekend. You had enough going on, don't you agree?"

"No, I don't agree." Mara felt anger rising up her neck. "I can't believe you'd put someone in management without my approval. Do you realize you've effectively chopped out part of my job?"

"Right," his voice held a tinge of exasperation. "That's the point — to free you up to do what you do best."

Her back stiffened. "Who are you to decide what I do best? Are you saying I'm not running my company well?"

"Of course you're good at your job. I think you're meant for bigger things than the tedium of —"

"Tedium!" Her face darkened into a wall of thunderclouds. "I have a dream and you seem bent on taking it all away, not helping me achieve it."

"Mara," he gentled his voice and reached out for her, "that's David's dream, not yours."

Mara put distance between them. "It was, I mean, is . . . ours." She sat down on her large exercise ball prescribed by the physical therapist as a new desk chair.

"Really? Then why do you tense up, get irritable, and have heart palpitations when you sit down at that desk? Why does your whole body say you hate doing financials and dealing with human resources?"

Mara stayed rock still as she tried hard to relax her shoulders. She couldn't do it. She closed her eyes and let her breath out in a whoosh. "I made David a promise." Heavy, round tears slid down her cheeks.

Anyone else would have relegated the big, blue exercise ball to the far corner. But not Mara. She'd made a commitment to use it in place of the office chair. Joel knew once she gave her word, she managed the decision, but never considered reneging. Never. How could he help Mara see she needed to break this promise to protect her health and honor the calling on her life? Her heart and soul were breaking more every day she kept this one. It would go against all she stood for, but changing the way she viewed her role with Bridger Pack and Rescue was the one thing that would free Mara from captivity. The choice she should have made years ago when David convinced her to give up her God-given dreams for his. Could she let go of what kept her from living out God's will for her life or would she stay in bondage to someone else's dream? Someone else's plan? "When did David become your idol?"

Mara's face registered shock. She stood and walked to the window. She kept her back to him. Her words were heavy, dark, measured. "I promised. I don't break promises."

Joel picked up the ball. "You promised? You promised to dedicate your life to misery? I don't think that's what David wanted." He heaved the ball out the door. It bounced off the wall of Jill's office and sprang right back into the room. "Sometimes promises are made without recognition of the consequences, without wisdom, with too much emphasis on the emotions. Sometimes promises should be broken in order to follow God's will and not our own because we made a promise God didn't ask us to make." The ball rolled to a stop at his feet. He kicked it back out of the way.

"How in the world did you come up with that conclusion? God wouldn't ask me to break my promises! God's honorable, at least I think He's supposed to be." Did she mean to say that? In her spirit she knew the truth. God hadn't broken his promise to her, but she had been trying to best God at his own game. Mara's stomach churned. Who did she think she was trying to be better than God?

"Mara, listen. I read an old story once about a man, Jephthah, who wanted to win a battle so badly he promised the first thing that greeted him on his arrival home as a burnt sacrifice. He won the battle. He kept the Israelites from being overrun and enslaved. The victory was stupendous and unbelievable with the odds his warriors faced. They conquered over twenty towns that would have conquered Jephthah's people. The victorious army went home as heroes."

He took a few steps toward Mara and touched her shoulder, willing her to turn to him.

She stepped aside to force his hand to drop.

"On his arrival home, the first thing that greeted Jephthah was his daughter, his only child. Jephthah couldn't celebrate though he'd saved the Israelites. He spent years mourning over the sacrifice of his daughter instead."

He saw a little break in her stance as Mara dipped her head downward.

"Do you think God asked Jephthah for that vow? Do you think Jephthah regretted his promise made in the intense emotion of the moment? And yet he carried it out. Mara, the story of an emotional promise that seems good at the time is in the Bible to warn us away from ill-advised vows. In the deepest part of my heart, I do not believe God wanted Jephthah to sacrifice his daughter. I don't think God even wanted the promise at all. And I don't think we are to hold onto decisions that take us away from God's will or down paths that cause destruction to anyone we love or ourselves."

She shook her head. "I can't deal with this right now, Joel."

"Why not, Mara? What you're doing by refusing to delegate is a psychological form of hoarding. Do you really think God will hold you accountable for a promise made that takes you out of his will for you just because you comforted a dying man with your words?"

Mara turned around and stared at him as if he'd struck her face.

Joel kept his hands to himself though he itched to reach out again. He wanted to soothe her, comfort her, or shake some sense into her. He could intentionally give Mara the position of power or lose all he'd worked for the last several weeks. He needed her to be sure she made the choice without another man dictating the outcome. He'd ask, but this was her choice. "Mara, please consider —"

"Joel, I understand what you're saying. But what about Isaac? God asked Abraham to sacrifice his only child, Isaac."

His gut twisted. Isaac. His mind raced to

remember the Old Testament story. *God, help me to help her. Give me your words, not my own.* "Yes, to test him. But then God provided the sacrifice. He sent a ram and never asked Abraham to carry out the promise. Abraham looked up and saw a ram caught in the thicket. All he had to do was accept the new opportunity when the Lord provided another way. I think God's provided another way for you too, Mara."

"What other way?"

"Me. I'm your ram. He's put me right in front of you to offer an alternative opportunity. I've been praying about this and I have an idea."

Mara almost smiled as she said, "Ah, I'm supposed to sacrifice you?" She rolled her lips in and held a straight face for all of a second before little creases formed around her eyes and mouth.

Joel laughed at her unexpected humor. "In a way. I think you've laid down your Isaac. Now it's time to accept a gift."

She stayed quiet as she mulled over his words. "I don't know, Joel. I started this business with David. I have obligations." Even as she said it, Joel watched her posture slump. If joy were a balloon, hers hissed a leak.

"How long will you continue to live like this?"

Mara's attention riveted back on Joel. "What do you mean?"

"Mara, everything about you screams you hate numbers. Don't get me wrong. You're good at it. You're sure smart enough to do any of it, all of it." He took her hand in his. "But you hate it. Am I way off base here?"

She blew out a steady stream of air as if she counted to ten before she responded. "I feel trapped when I stare at numbers all day."

"How can it be God's will to shackle you to a desk? You are so alive and vibrant when working on Cadence's quilt or helping people learn to express themselves through art. Your excitement, your energy . . ." He shook his head. "When you're in the creative element, you glow. When you're stuck with the numbers, you fade like the valley after sundown. I've literally watched you wilt."

"I don't know what to do." Mara's free hand smoothed across her cheek and her little pinky rubbed circles across an eyelid until she held her face for comfort.

If he could gather Mara up and hold her, he would. But she had to come to this decision without more emotion muddying the waters. "This is killing you. You, having this life — is killing you. Stop doing it. What if you fulfilled David's dream by selling the business?

Mara's head snapped up. "You're just —"

Joel spread his hands out wide in front of his chest. "Whoa. No. No, Mara, I'm not." *Big Guy, are you helping me here? I don't know how to say it alone.* "Don't you get it? I lo—." He swallowed the last word. Now was not the time to share his feelings. Not in the heat of a life-changing argument. But he couldn't stop the heat of his words. "You don't understand because you're so wrapped up in keeping a promise like Jeph-thah! What if there were a way to help the business continue but you don't have to be the one managing the financial details, hir-ing, firing, and dealing with contracts?"

"I knew it. You do want my company!" Her eyes narrowed as she realized how deeply he'd betrayed her. "Spouting Bible stories at me! I welcomed you into my fam-ily. You've been included in sacred events! You've been manipulating me and using God to do it, haven't you?" She stomped to the door. "I'm an idiot, but you're low."

"Mara, of course not." He followed her and tried to take her hand. "You need to be the front person, designing and teaching. Just hire the right people. Let me handle it

268

for you so you can move on."

"Move on." She pulled back with a horrified expression. He'd said those same words about Louie. "Just get rid of me like my dog and move on?" She ripped the door back further and pointed out. "This is my company, not yours. You're fired!"

Mara stabbed the embroidery needle in and out of the last quilt block forming the words Made in Montana in champagne silk thread. The ladies from church were due any minute to finish putting the top together with her.

"Mom, are you killing it or sewing it?" Toby asked as he walked through the living room.

"I'll let you know," she grumbled and jabbed the final stitch through.

He gave her a surprised look and scooted into the kitchen fast.

Mara unlocked the embroidery ring and held up the quilt block. She analyzed it with a critical eye. The snow castle photo Cadence snapped a few days earlier disappeared into the white poplin. She'd need to stitch a border to help it stand out from the white-on-white. But Joel stood out in the center focus. His head tipped back in carefree splendor. The timer caught both the snowball she'd let fly and their joyous faces. It also caught Toby's surprised flail down the slide and Marisa's impish delight set off by Cadence's hilarious dive away from his feet.

Toby ran back from the kitchen with a sandwich, avoiding Mara, as he headed toward his room. She watched him with a sense of guilt.

Cadence and Marisa came through the front door. "Hey, Mom." They sang out in unison. Boots went flying off into the corner.

Mara forced brevity into her voice. "Hi, girls."

Marisa plunked down on the sofa as Cadence turned the corner. "So when's Superman getting here for dinner?"

Mara didn't look up from the quilt block. His face in the picture. That's all she'd see of him from now on. She had to come clean with the kids though. "He's not coming."

"Huh? He always comes for dinner."

"Not anymore. I'm sorry." She mumbled, "I had to let him go."

Cadence flipped back around. "What? What do you mean you let Joel go?"

Toby ran down the hall. "You fired Joel?"

Mara sighed. "Look, we had a disagreement and there wasn't a solution we could agree on."

"That's lame, Mom." Marisa's lips quivered.

"Look, this isn't up for discussion. I did what I had to do."

Toby shook his head. "I just played hoops with him last night. Nothing was wrong then."

Mara took on a stern demeanor. She didn't want to yell at the kids, but she was coming close to losing control. "Again, this is an adult matter. It is not up for discussion."

Cadence's eyes bored into Mara's. Her anger sparked across the room until she looked at her sister's sadness. Cadence put an arm around Marisa. "You blew it big, Mom." The girls walked out of the living room silent and downcast.

Toby slapped his hands against his sides and went back to his room.

"Yeah, I know," she whispered to herself. The joy in the photo block slammed her between the eyes. She didn't want to see what her temper had destroyed. Mara balled up the quilt block and stuffed it to the bottom of the pile.

What was she thinking? She'd use the church ski retreat she'd already made before Cadence added the snow castle. Joel wasn't in her family and it didn't make any sense to use a block with him in it.

The doorbell rang and Mara's home filled with ladies laden with their potluck dishes and enthusiasm.

"I've been looking forward to this," Lisa told Mara.

"Me too. I've really enjoyed it."

"You've been teaching us so much! Why didn't you become a teacher?" Lisa asked. "You're a natural the way you can explain the details and guide us."

Mara's brows drew together. "I used to dream of teaching art and design. I guess life just went another way."

"Well, it's never too late to follow your dreams." Lisa smiled at her and went to help set out food.

Mara didn't want to think about how closely Lisa's words echoed Joel's. God seemed to be sending her repetitive messages. She peeked up toward heaven. *Is that what's going on here, God? Did Joel see the same thing Lisa did?* She groaned. *Oh, please, don't let me have made that mistake!*

Before they all left, Mara took a picture of the finished quilt top and then another of all the ladies she'd been teaching to share on her website. Except for her thoughts of Joel, she'd had a perfect night.

18

"What is it you want to change on the military exhibition team uniforms and packs?" Mara rubbed her temples as she listened to the speakerphone. The lack of sleep since she'd fired Joel yesterday gave her a headache. She couldn't tell if the irritability crawling up her backbone sizzled under the surface from the night of no sleep or the replays of their argument raging in her head. Lisa's idea of teaching art and design kept popping into her mind at odd moments too, like a buzzing fly that wouldn't go away.

"I've been on your website and blog this morning and noticed you can do specialized designs that mimic stained glass. Are these new?" Her government contact sounded very impressed.

"I've been working those designs into quilts, but they're not for gear." Mara mentally kicked herself for that blog post.

"That's the border for my daughter's gradu-ation quilt in various stages of production. I'm thinking of adding a new division."

"What can you do with that design for us?"

"What do you mean? We already agreed on designs."

"Don't get me wrong, the designs you provided are beautiful and functional, but the originality I see in those quilts would appeal to the public. It's sharp, stark, and eye-catching. We'll keep the camouflage designs for the service uniforms as is for the team's on-duty rescue missions. Remember the performance uniforms can be a lot more visually creative. We mean to educate and entertain. I think incorporating eye-catching designs like those would take the stage pres-ence of the team to the next level. Don't you?"

"I've only used those on quilting patterns, not packs and uniforms. I don't think they'd be quite right." Mara picked up a drawing pencil and started doodling a possible idea.

"Why don't you try? We want something memorable and striking to really wow the crowds. Like the quilt. It wowed me. I'd love the packs for both uniforms to be the same design, but the service packs for actual rescue still have to be in the camouflage colors. Can you make a solid navy blue uniform with accents that match a rescue pack with red, white, and blue stained glass effects?"

Mara studied her skimpy sketch. "Maybe. I could use the same navy material as the soldering effect between white and red. The packs could use larger pieces, but the handwork on all the pieces would add labor cost. You realize this enacts the change clause in our contract."

"I understand. We're fine with the change clause. The cost is still within budget."

She wobbled the pencil back and forth over her thumb and watched the bending magical illusion she'd learned in elementary school. "How long can you give me to work this out?"

"Two days. We can extend the time with the change clause enacted by two days."

Mara choked. "If I get a design for all the gear, the packs, and the K-9s in time then do we get an extension on delivery? I have to reset all my machines and —"

"If you're as good as your promise, then you'll deliver on time. Our performance schedule doesn't change. It's set in stone, barring natural disaster. These dates have been confirmed for a year in advance."

"But —." Now would be an excellent time

to have Joel managing the shop for her so she could . . . Mara whipped her traitorous thoughts back into place.

"I thought you could handle this contract, Mrs. Keegan."

"Yes, I can. We'll manage. You'll get the designs as soon as possible for approval. Then I'll need your signed change order back immediately in order to meet the deadline. Agreed?"

"I look forward to seeing the new designs." A short silence on the line and then she said, "Have you ever thought about teaching what you do? Your artistic talent is quite unique and you are well-spoken."

"Thank you." She hung up. What in the world was going on with all the direct suggestions? Teaching? Mara's spirit clicked again. She battled it down. The last thing she needed right now with the change order would be to mentally play with ideas she might one day do. Her brain spun with possible solutions to her sudden time deficit. In order to meet this newest challenge, she'd have to spend every minute of the next two days with the utmost efficiency. There'd be no time for her kids, regular meals, or a decent night's sleep if she didn't delegate a good portion of her work. There certainly wasn't time to dream about ideas like adding customer design classes to her schedule.

Without Joel, what used to be a spectacular success dropped into the dust bunny nest under her desk. She wasn't incapable, but taking back the finances and reassigning Constance might not have been her smartest move. Payroll and monthly taxes had to get done. So did this new change order. She needed help.

Mara hung her head in shame. She needed to admit Joel was right and apologize to both Constance and Joel. The easiest first. She might build the courage she needed to face Joel. "Jill, would you page Constance and ask her to come see me, please?" The clock taunted her with its rhythmic tick-tock.

Toby picked at his food in front of the TV. Cadence took hers to the computer room under the guise of homework. Only Marisa sat at the dining room table with Mara. Even a spiced roast beef, a family favorite, couldn't coax them into a little bit of normal. Joel's empty chair somehow shouted to be filled by a live body. Two empty chairs took three times the coping effort. Losing David taught her to cope with grief by simple means. Live the next moment. Then the next. One breath after the next. One minute to the next built to an hour. Get through the next minute.

"When's Superman coming back?" Marisa watched her mother with accusation.

Mara put her forkful of roast beef down and swallowed the lump in her throat. "Honey, I don't know. I put a call in to his office, but he hasn't called back yet."

"Why'd you do it, Mom?" Marisa's question came with a whispered hitch. "It's like our whole lives just fell apart. No Dad, no Louie, and now no Joel either." She started to cry.

Own it. She had to own this mistake before she could possibly solve it. If it were solvable. "Because I blew it, GirlieQ. Sometimes we just blow it big." Mara plopped her elbow on the table and rested her chin in her hand. "I'm so sorry." A pool gathered behind her eyes too.

Marisa nodded as a tear slipped down her nose. "He kinda fit in like he was s'posed to be here. I asked God to let you be happy again."

"Oh Marisa, honey —"

"We all did, you know, pray. All us kids. We figured maybe the Big Guy sent Joel to help us be more like a family like we used to be."

Mara's throat constricted. Her kids loved

him too. *Whoa!*

"He kept staying like he was meant to be here." She didn't bother to eat the meat. Marisa bounced the fork off it like a trampoline. "Then you fired him. Why?"

Mara sat up. The best way to deal with a thirteen-year-old's inquisition was to tell the straight truth. Otherwise, she'd never feel the necessity of truth in her own life. All Mara could think or see was the blinding white of an emotional avalanche.

"I let my fear about the business Daddy and I built get in the way of logic, love, and wisdom. Sometimes it's better to walk away and talk out your emotions before acting on them. I should have done that. I should have talked it out with someone I trusted. Instead I let my emotions make me irrational."

"Did you say you are sorry to him? I forgave you. Wouldn't he?"

The sweetness of her daughter's immediate forgiveness touched Mara. If only the adult world were so simple. "Not yet. I mean he'd probably forgive me, but I don't know if he'll come back." Mara lowered her gaze. Talk about accountability. Her daughter didn't miss a bit. "I tried to call but he hasn't returned my calls."

"Call again." Marisa's tone and look reminded Mara of the comedian who says,

"Here's your sign."

It was stupid. She should wear a sign that read, "My emotions won, that's why I lost."

"I can't. It would be a bit creepy to keep calling."

"Yeah," Toby called in from the sofa, "I guess you don't need to turn into some stalker weirdo."

Stalker weirdo. One job description she'd never thought of for herself and yet she'd toyed with calling and calling until Joel finally picked up and answered. The weight of her error built a sense of guilt she couldn't wait to release.

Cadence walked out of the hallway balancing dishes still covered in food. "What if you wrote him an apology? Like send him a letter."

"I suppose I could do that. At least he might open the letter." If his whole office didn't already know, they would if she sent a personal letter. "But what if someone else got it first?" The last question was more for Mara's thinking than the response to Cadence.

"Do you have another way of contacting him?" Cadence stopped and set her plate, cup, and silverware on the table. "Wait. I have a better idea. Let's get a ticket for the Museum Ball. You can invite him to attend with you. You guys were working on the donations before he left. You could say you need his help or something."

"Oh, yeah, you got it." Marisa held her hand up for a high five from Cadence. They slapped hands.

"That's a little much, don't you think?" Mara waved a hand through the air. "I fired him and then I'm all of a sudden sending an invitation to a fund-raiser gala and asking for fluff info?" She shook her head. "I'll send the note if he doesn't call back. Okay?"

The girls looked at each other. "Nope," they said in unison. Marisa ran for a note card from the embossed stationery she'd received for Christmas. "I knew I needed to keep this stuff for something special."

Cadence handed her mother a pen. "So tell him, like, you're sorry first. That you've had time to think and —"

Mara lifted her brows. "Cadence, I can handle this part." Mara opened the blank note card. She wrote a simple, "I'm sorry." Then followed it with a request to talk. It felt too bland, too inane for the heat of the dismissal. She added a request for his forgiveness. Better to make sure she'd said everything in case this was her last chance. In all likelihood, Joel would toss the card without opening it anyway. She'd thrown him out of her office like a bad dog. She'd humiliated him. But what if he did read it?

"You know, I bet he's wondering how my midterm math test went. He helped me so much," Marisa said. "You better tell him that. And tell him I said thanks!"

"Hey, can you tell him we won the last game?" Toby asked. "He shot baskets with me till our arms dropped off. He'd like that, too."

"You can tell him my senior project got picked for the news spotlight," added Cadence.

How intricately involved in her life and the kids' lives Joel had become. He wasn't just interested in taking her company. This level of caring wasn't about money or business. Maybe he really was interested in her and her family. "I'm gonna need more paper."

"Joel!" Marisa shouted with glee.

He heard a commotion on the other end of the line as Cadence grappled with Marisa over the phone. He tried to ease the tension between the girls and spoke up louder to get their attention. "Hey, how's it going?" The sound of feet running away clip-clopped down the hall. He could see it in his mind. The long hall, the living room, the family in the house. He missed them all deeply.

Cadence came on the phone. "Joel, did you get Mom's note?"

"As a matter of fact —"

Marisa launched herself into the call on the other extension. "Did you? Did you get it? We sent it two days ago and the post office guy said you'd get it today."

Well, at least he knew they missed him, too. Marisa's eager voice warmed his heart. "I did, Marisa, and I thought I ought to call and talk with your mom. I tried to call her cell, but it went straight to voice mail. Is she at home?"

Cadence jumped back in, "No. She's redesigning uniforms for that military contract. You know the rescue dogs and all?"

"You're kidding me. Why is she doing that?"

"Some lady called. She saw the quilt pictures Mom put up on her website. And she put up a picture of the framing on my quilt. So this lady says she wants something like that on uniforms now."

Joel whistled. "Your mom must be really stressed."

"Yeah, you could say that." The laugh didn't quite ring with humor.

"Joel?" Marisa broke in. "Are you coming

to the ball?"

"Well, I thought I'd talk to your mom about that first. I should make sure she wants me there."

"Oh, she wants you there all right." The confidence in Marisa's statement took Joel off guard.

"She does? I know there's a ticket, but I think we need to figure out some details."

Cadence interrupted Marisa as she started to speak, "Marisa, hang on. I have an idea. Joel, we've had a family talk. We already know Mom said she was sorry in the note."

"I can see that." Joel smiled into the phone. He held up the note with all the kids' additional messages. "I can't tell you all how much it meant to me to hear how things are working out. The test, the game, and congratulations on your senior project, Cadence. Very cool stuff here."

"Well, what I was thinking might be even more cool," Cadence added.

"I'm listening."

"What do you think about surprising Mom at the Museum Ball? You know, like, show up and be wearing a tux. You could bring her flowers or something to show you forgive her. It would be better in person than a phone call by a million miles. Right?"

"I think we should at least —"

Marisa could hold her silence no longer. "Please, Joel. We could make it really special. It'd be the happiest thing to happen to Mom in a long time. She's been in a really bad mood since you left."

"She has?" Did she miss him the way he missed her? Or did she want to mend business ties?

"We already know she wants you to come. And you can, too, since you're holding a ticket, dude."

"I can't argue that point." Thirteen-year old logic made a lot of sense. Joel hoped he wasn't making a dumb decision. He hoped Mara forgave him fully, as her note said, but possibly also would open her heart as well. What would happen if he showed up at the ball as a surprise? Did Mara like surprises? One more thing he hoped to learn about the woman he loved.

19

Mara glanced in the full-length mirror on the back of her bedroom door. Her eyes looked smokey and wide. The lipstick Cadence found, a rich candy apple red, went well with her red velvet dress. Marisa's spray wax worked and her long, heavy hair seemed to hold the spiral curls Cadence gathered up into a waterfall cascade. She loved the results of all the girl-time.

Marisa giggled all afternoon about a special secret while Cadence constantly shushed her little sister. Mara wished the mystery would take her mind off the lack of communication from Joel. Maybe Cadence was ready to introduce a boy. That would be fun. Cadence hadn't done a lot of dating in high school. Her dad's death seemed to overshadow the desire to meet boys. Mara worried about her daughter's overfocus on family duties to the exclusion of the normal high school life.

"You girls look gorgeous." She gave each a hug, careful to protect their hair and make-up.

"You do, too, Mom," Cadence smiled.

"So, is there a boy meeting us there or not?" She winked at Marisa who covered another giggle.

"Oh, we'll see." With a coy glance over her shoulder, Cadence swished out of the bedroom. Marisa followed her sister out, but stopped to blow a kiss through the door.

Mara caught the kiss in the air and pressed it to her heart. She turned back to the mirror. And touched the fading welt. Her five-plus-week-old wound looked more like a thick marker stroke from a distance. She draped a black lace shawl in several different styles. None seemed right for the long velvet sleeves on the dress. The scar was a part of her now and she needed to come to terms with it. She'd use the scar to talk to people about heart health. God saw fit to allow the heart attack and valve repair in her life. She'd use the experience to touch the lives around her.

Mara tossed the shawl on her bed. Instead she chose a large sparkling diamond pendant and matching earrings from her jewelry case. David had given them to her for their tenth anniversary. She smiled as she thought of him. He'd approve of their use for a conversation starter, especially if it helped save a life. "Lord, let this scare be used for your glory. Draw someone to me tonight who really needs to hear how important it is to take care of our hearts both spiritually and physically. And, God? If you see fit, if it's in your will, please help Joel to forgive me and come back. Thank you."

Joel arrived early in a well-cut black tux. He preferred the long tie rather than the traditional bow tie. He hoped Mara would approve. He hoped Mara wouldn't have him escorted out of the building for not calling!

Pink, green, and blue lights alternately washed the entry to the museum. The huge projection of the Northern Lights displayed the evening's theme with grandeur.

Joel walked the long red carpet and waited inside the festive lobby for the kids to arrive. Inside, the decor reflected the theme creatively. Recessed ceiling lighting glowed a soft blue, hanging lights held green bulbs, and each gallery entrance had beautiful pink fairy strands draped around the door frames.

Joel caught sight of Marisa as she stood at the beginning of the long red carpet. She looked like a porcelain doll with her beautiful dark hair curled into a side clip and spilled over her lemon yellow dress.

Then came an even more stunning young woman. Joel almost didn't recognize Cadence. Her Grecian-styled gown flowed around her as she moved.

Toby remembered his manners and offered an elbow to each sister. He sported a new haircut that turned him from an unkempt-looking mop to a well-groomed teen.

"Joel!" Marisa called him over. The kids all swarmed him with hugs.

Toby, Marisa, and Cadence found their station and took coats for guests.

"Where's your mom?" Joel craned his neck over the kids to see the entry. "Does she need help?"

Cadence responded with a pat on his arm. "She'll be here. No worries, Superman. We asked you here early because we have to check coats for the school fund-raiser. We wanted to be sure you showed."

"You were worried?"

"Well, yeah," Marisa said with a blush. "We kinda didn't let you talk to Mom."

Toby added, "We thought you might chicken out. Okay, I did after these two told me what they planned."

Joel smiled. "I admit it's a little risky, but

I wouldn't have missed it."

"We did a makeover on her. You are going to be very impressed." She elbowed Marisa. "Right?"

"She looks so good." Marisa looked proud of herself. "We even got her to let us curl her hair."

A moment later Mara appeared, framed by the white chain link that ran the length of the red carpet walkway. The red velvet gown skimmed her shoulders and followed the lovely line of her figure. The slight flare at her knees emphasized the curve of her hips. She wore one intense sparkling necklace with a teardrop pendant and matching teardrop earrings. The stone in the necklace sat just above her scar.

Joel couldn't take his eyes off her. He hadn't seen her out of a comfortable sweat suit in a month. Joel sucked in his breath. Rich called it right. No, helping Mara with the business wasn't his reason for staying in Bozeman.

She walked at a slow pace. Anyone not aware of her recent broken ankle would think her pace graceful. Mara's subtle movement added a hint of mystery as the velvet flowed around her legs. Her elegant, slow glide drew every eye in the room and the many new arrivals behind her. The small black satin clutch bag in her hand matched the black ballet slippers that peeked out from under the hem of her dress.

Joel's mouth went dry and his mind blanked.

"Joel?" Cadence tapped his shoulder.

"What?"

"I told you she'd knock his socks off." Cadence laughed. "You guys have dishes and kitchen duty the next two days."

Joel still didn't look away from Mara's approach. "Huh?"

"She looks great, doesn't she?"

He coughed. "Yes, yes she does." Not that she didn't every day, but tonight he saw a new side of Mara. A side of femininity she'd kept hidden. Joel's heart pounded at the sight of a beautiful, intelligent woman he knew he loved. But now he needed to know she wanted more than a coach.

She smiled and her face lit up as she caught sight of him. With that moment, a fire lit deep inside his heart. Then she reached out for his hand. "Thank you for coming." The fire leapt from his fingertips across the space between them. The magnetic current fused their hands together. Mara's eyes widened. He knew right then she felt it, too. Joel couldn't lift his gaze from Mara's ruby red lips.

Toby cleared his throat. "So, like, we're going to head over to the coat check."

Somewhere in Joel's head, he heard Toby and nodded.

Mara's left arm tingled. This time not from a heart attack. A barrage of emotion zinged through her veins then zapped the strength from her knees. She swayed toward Joel.

He bent his mouth close to her ear to be heard over the live band. "Would you like to dance?"

Her mouth was dry. Her voice came out husky. "Yes."

Joel released her fingers and slipped a hand on the small of Mara's back. The warmth of his hand spread a sense of security. A little tremor shivered up from his touch on her back.

Mara looked up into Joel's face as he guided her onto the dance floor. His eyes drew her into his presence as if there were no other people in the room. More than forgiveness, she saw desire as if he wanted to kiss her.

Joel's hard bicep flexed under her hand as they danced. Mara blinked as she realized how intimate her thoughts ran about this man.

He leaned in again. His voice silky smooth

blew a light breath through her hair. "Can we talk after the benefit?"

Mara nodded. Somehow she'd been tongue-tied more in the last few minutes than ever in her life. The tux fit his shoulders and accentuated his athletic physique. She wanted to lean into his arms and lay her head on those strong shoulders. What would it feel like to be enclosed in his embrace right now?

The music ended and the emcee suggested attendees peruse the auction tables.

Mara didn't want to lose contact with Joel. When he took her hand in his, she smiled at him.

They strolled to the beautiful exhibition of auction items. The line of white tablecloths glowed from underneath in ever-changing colors of the aurora borealis. Fiber optic centerpieces chased the pinks, greens, blues, and whites of the night sky up and down their fronds. Ski packages, jewelry, dinners with celebrities all sounded glamorous and exciting.

Mara stopped at Spire Climbing Center's prize package. Six climbers could have an instructor for an hour-and-a-half. "What a perfect birthday present for Toby!"

Mara listed her bid number and an amount on the sheet. Then she tapped it with the pen. "I'm going to have to watch that one."

"He'll love it. I hope you get it for him," Joel agreed. "Did you see the Yellowstone tour in the brochure?"

"Mammoth? Yes. That would be an awesome adventure."

"Haven't you been to Yellowstone?" Joel asked.

"We took the kids camping there when they were really little." She shrugged. "But we were too busy building the business to go again. And we've never stayed in a lodge or taken the snowcoach tours."

"I've always wanted to go in and stay to explore." Joel explained, "My folks took me through Yellowstone in a car when I was about ten. But other than the photo op stops, we just did a drive-through."

"You should bid on one of the packages."

"Maybe." He looked into her eyes. "But I'd need someone to go with."

She couldn't help herself. The words popped out. "I'd go with you."

He squeezed her hand. "Maybe we could arrange that."

As they continued through the displays, Mara mentally kicked herself for being so blatant. Who knew where this would lead? She couldn't go promising to visit Yellowstone on overnights with him. But every time she looked into his eyes, she saw forever. And he did come back.

Once they had a chance to talk out the argument, they could decide where to go from here. Mara snuck a side-glance at Joel. She'd like to go somewhere from here.

"Okay, here's a fun one!" Joel laughed. "Sapphire mining. Do you think anyone ever finds a gem?"

Mara pointed at the description. "For the price, they'd better. But it's Montana Yogo sapphires. They're my favorite stones."

"Really?"

"Chalk it up to my being a native Montanan, literally." She teased with a wink.

"Shall we go mining?" He leaned down and signed his bid number on the sheet. "I'm up for the adventure."

They added bids to a few more items on their wish lists.

Mara tapped Joel's shoulder as he turned to look at another lineup of auction items. "I think we better sit down before we spend both our incomes in one night."

He guided her through the spectacular Museum Ball decor to the Bridger Pack and Rescue table she'd agreed to as a Silver Sponsor. Bigger fiber optic centerpieces sat on all the tables. Oval mirrors reflected light up from beneath each display. Net lights twinkled like Northern Light curtain formations from strategic spots around the main gallery in pink, green, blue, and white.

"It's gorgeous!" Mara said as she looked all around. "I love how they've added more and more as we go deeper into the museum."

Jill and her husband, Constance and her date all stood as they arrived.

The private bubble around Mara and Joel dissipated. All Mara wanted was to get it back. She couldn't wait for the evening to end.

Joel moved away from Mara to shake hands with the men.

Jill came around the table and hugged Mara. "I'm so glad you're here." She whispered, "And wow! No other words, lady, wow!"

Jill's gaze dropped to Mara's scar. "Does it still hurt?"

Mara never felt self-conscious before. But this was new territory. "Not much at all. Okay, if I sneeze it's not so great."

"You're really okay?"

"I'm almost feeling back to normal." She stepped back to see Jill's dress. "That royal blue is beautiful on you. Makes your eyes pop."

"Thanks." She pointed at her husband chatting with the other men. "I made him get all gussied up too. You should have heard the whining."

They laughed.

Constance held out a hand. "Good to see you out and about. Thank you for the tickets." Her dress was a simple black sheath. She looked lovely. There was no hint of animosity over the fast position changes.

Mara took her hand and squeezed it. "No, Constance, thank you for coming tonight. I don't know how I'd have finished those new designs in time without you."

"Just doing my job." She smiled. "I'm glad everything worked out. I want to be an asset to you. This is a great place to start networking." She winked. "I need to learn more about my new community."

"Music to my ears." Not a hint of tension. Relief released through Mara. "I'm happy you decided to stay after my rough start with you."

"I think we'll do just fine." Constance turned to Joel. "Don't you, Joel?"

He spread his hands wide. "Hey, I'm leaving it up to the lady in charge."

Mara smiled. "I think you did a great job finding Constance. Thank you."

The music swelled into a new song. The

other couples left the table to join the crowded dance floor.

Joel held out his hand. "Are you up to some more dancing?"

"A nice slow one and we'll call it good. Okay?" She tapped her leg. "After last weekend's snow excursion, I'm going to let my muscles build back a little more slowly."

She placed her hand on his palm. Joel's fingers closed around hers.

"Was the day too much for you?"

Mara reassured Joel, "I'm fine. But using muscles I hadn't used for a while made me realize I need to be a little more gradual with my excursions."

"One dance and then we'll get one of those fun photos over there."

"We don't need a photo," Mara said.

"Of course we do. This is a monumental moment."

"It is?"

"Yes, it is."

"Okay, I'm game. Why is this a monumental moment?"

"Because it's one you will never want to forget." He winked and smiled into her eyes.

She smiled back, but said nothing more. *You're right about that, Joel Ryan, you're right about that.* Mara let Joel sweep her into the swirl of the crowd.

■ ■ ■ ■

"May I escort you home?" Joel asked.

"I have my car here."

"What if I follow you over to some place we can get a cup of coffee or a soda?

Mara didn't want the sweetness of the evening to end. But she was nervous. In order for them to build a relationship, they needed to have one short talk and clear the air. What if the talk didn't turn out well? Then what? The only way she'd get past this sense of being in a holding tank would be to have the talk.

She took a steadying breath. "Yes, I'd like that."

"Do you have something warmer to wear? It's pretty chilly out there."

"In the car."

"Give me your valet ticket. I can have the valet bring it in and your car will be all warmed up for you."

Mara handed him the ticket. "Thank you."

As he walked out the door, Marisa walked over swinging her new gold strappy sandals.

"Hey, GirlieQ." Mara put an arm around her.

"Hey, Mama. How's it going with Superman? You guys all fixed up?" She yawned.

Mara smiled. Not too long ago she'd have carried Marisa home and tucked her into bed with a stuffed kitty named Meowzers.

"I think we're going to go have a chat now."

"Yes-s-s." Marisa made a victory fist.

"Hang on and let's see what comes."

Cadence and Toby joined them.

"What're you all amped up for?" Toby asked his little sister.

Toby's suit jacket was off, his tie stuffed in the shirt pocket, and the top button opened on the dress shirt.

Mara teased, "Didn't take you two long to undo your fancy duds."

Cadence still looked perfectly put together. "They're just lightweights."

Toby laughed at her, then taunted, "But I don't have to impress Mr. Cupcake over there."

"Shh!" Cadence looked quickly at the young man helping check out the final bidders to see if he'd heard the brotherly ribbing.

"Mr. Cupcake?" Mara asked.

Cadence took on a dreamy look. "He brought me a mini cupcake at the coat check and asked if I wanted to go to the Taylor Planetarium grand opening next week."

She waved to the dark-haired boy and he waved back.

"Now Toby's calling him Mr. Cupcake." She smiled sweetly at her brother and then stomped on his toe.

"Ow!" He jumped back. "Oh, now it's Mr. Mini-cupcake!"

Cadence turned her back toward the auction collections table and growled under her breath. "Try it and I'll get your other toe."

Joel brought a whoosh of cold air with him as he entered the building. "Hey gang, may I have your permission to take your mom on a coffee date?"

All three settled right down at his request.

Marisa answered first. "Told ya my prayers would work."

Cadence put her hand over Marisa's mouth and edged her toward the door. "We'll see you at home, Mom."

"Uh, yeah. See you there." Toby limped away with an exaggerated flair.

"Ready?" Joel held out Mara's black faux fur evening jacket.

"Thank you." She slipped her arms in and zipped the rhinestone zipper. The satin lining along the collar brushed softly against her chin.

"Let's go have that talk. Where to?"

"We could go to Montana Ale Works. It's

just two or three miles away." She held out her skirt. "We'd be less out of place than a twenty-four-hour diner."

"Sounds great. I'll follow you."

A few minutes later, Mara and Joel walked into a very crowded restaurant of formally dressed people.

He looked around at the historic building admiring the restoration. "It looks like everyone from the Museum Ball had the same idea," Joel said as they followed the hostess to the less crowded overflow seating.

"I think that worked out well, don't you?" She slid into her seat in the antique railroad car.

Though dark out, the city lights around them glistened. "Great view." Joel appreciated the romantic spot for what he had in mind tonight. He couldn't have found a better place for what he hoped would come from their talk.

They watched light traffic drive by on Main Street until the waiter came for their order. Once placed, Joel reached across the table for Mara's hand.

"Listen, I want you to feel comfortable with me. I need you to know I'm not now and will never be after Bridger Pack and

Rescue. The business — that's not why I came back."

Mara bit her lip. "Joel, can I tell you how sorry I am that my hot buttons got in the way? I should have let you explain. Instead, my emotions and fears took over."

His thumb rubbed her knuckles. "I know, Mara, I really do. Here comes the guy who almost ruined your business to coach you. I can see how it was hard for you to trust me. Then add the broken ankle, your heart surgery, and losing your beloved dog. I'm sorry I didn't tell you about Constance. I wanted to help you, not hurt you."

She nodded but kept her eyes on the table. "I appreciate that very much. I think I've just been so afraid the last few years that sometimes things feel bigger than they are."

"But we're bigger than all that." Joel ducked down to catch her attention. "At least I hope you think we are."

She looked up at him. "You do?"

"I do." Joel held his free hand out for Mara's.

She took it without reservation.

"God is in all this, like the quilt you're making. I couldn't see how all the pieces would come together in your quilt. As the designer, you could. But I have faith it's going to be gorgeous. God is designing something beautiful out of the mixed-up pieces in our lives. I have faith in God's plan for our relationship, too."

"We've certainly had a lot to overcome." She gave him a radiant smile. "The memories are special."

"Do you think you'd be willing to see a relationship with me as a valuable opportunity?"

"It's an opportunity I don't want to miss out on, Joel."

He stood and moved to her side of the table.

"Playing musical chairs on me, are you?" the waiter said as he delivered their drinks. "If I had a date half as pretty as yours, I'd be switching chairs, too."

They laughed with him.

"I'll be back to check on you folks in a bit."

Joel picked up Mara's hand again and held it to his heart. "Will you promise to give us a chance?"

Mara searched his face with her luminous brown eyes. "Yes," she finally answered, "but how in the world are we going to start seeing each other with you in another city?"

"I was hoping you'd ask that." He let go of her hand and wrapped an arm around her. "Since I coach by phone, for the time being I'll move my office up here. Maybe I can rent a room from Mrs. Calder again or find a small apartment."

"I'm sure Mrs. Calder will love having you back." Mara looked chagrined. "She wasn't too happy with me when you left suddenly. And let me tell you, the kids told her right away what they thought of it all, too."

Joel tossed his head back and guffawed. "You've raised some awesome kids, Mara."

She playfully hit his chest. "In case you didn't know it, I was quite a villain all week to pretty much everyone." She stopped talking and looked him squarely in the eye. "Wait a minute. Actually the kids all seemed a lot more mellow toward me since Thursday."

He cleared his throat and looked out at the night sky. He knew he'd been caught. Would she feel betrayed again?

"They knew, didn't they?" Her voice lilted softly and full of humor.

He released his breath. Whew! "If you put it that way . . ." Joel teased.

Mara shook her head. "My, my. You were all in cahoots."

"Because we all love you."

"You love me?" she whispered.

"I do. I love you." Joel dipped his head and kissed the ruby red lips he'd wanted to taste all night.

Mara pulled back. "I need to tell you one more thing."

"Anything."

"After we fill the government contract, I'm taking your advice. Bridger Pack and Rescue is adding a new division for design students."

"Mara, I'm thrilled for you. That's a great decision." He held back from his urge to coach.

"Thank you for showing me I needed a new management plan. I can see it's working and I'm open to whatever else it takes to make this business become what God intends. I want to honor the dreams God created me to achieve." She laid her palm on his cheek. "You helped me find me again. My art. The me I was meant to be. Thank you."

Joel's job satisfaction soared. But his heart leapt like the mountain goats up high and free. He leaned down and kissed Mara with all the joy in his being.

20

"There." Mara sat back and admired the finished quilt as Cadence walked into her workroom.

"Well, you look happy, Mom."

"It's all done." She ran both her hands across the surface as she searched for stray strings. "And it's beautiful, if I do say so myself."

Cadence looked up and down the quilt and examined every square. "What are you talking about? You can't be finished."

"Of course, I'm finished. See? I just have this little thread to clip —"

Cadence jumped in, "No way. Where's my snow cave picture? Joel has been a big part of our lives during my senior year. There's no way he doesn't have a picture on my quilt." She crossed her arms and planted her feet.

"But Cadence, Joel's not —"

"Joel's not what?" She cocked her head to

the side. "Not what, Mom?"

"Well he's not part of the family." Lame, she already knew the next word out of her daughter's mouth.

"Lame, Mom, lame."

"Cadence —"

"Seriously, Mom, what are you going to do to fix it? I want Joel on the quilt. We'd never have made it through this whole, this whole . . ." She unwrapped her arms and whipped her hands toward the ceiling. "This whole mess without Joel!"

Mara knew Cadence was right. She shouldn't have switched out the block without at least saying something to Cadence about it. But the quilt was finished with all the photos, squares, and pieces in place. She looked from the quilt to her furious daughter and back at the magnificent handiwork helped along by renewed friendships. The quilt was a spectacular thing of beauty.

"I don't know what to do, Cadence. I can't destroy this and redo it. How about I make another one?"

"No." Cadence upped her ante. "He should have been on more than one block."

"Well what can I do? Look, where would I put pictures of Joel even if I had them."

"You have some." She ran over to the

stack of paperwork and photos that piled higher and higher over the last weeks.

Papers flew in every direction. "Ah-hah! See?"

She turned around with an eight-by-ten and a few small snapshots. Cadence handed them to Mara. "Okay, so now what?"

Mara sorted through the snapshots. The kids had been busy! There were various shots of her family with Joel in a cafeteria, bleachers at the high school, and a few of all of them at the Museum Ball. "Is that the hospital cafeteria?" Mara pointed at the first picture.

"Yep." Cadence grinned. "We bonded and prayed to the Big Guy there for you to get well."

Mara looked up at Cadence, surprised. "Really?"

"Uh-huh. Joel was there constantly with us. He must have bought us a bazillion meals. But we never ate first. We always prayed first." Cadence's face took on a loving, soft expression. "Mom, I believe the Big Guy really loves me and you too."

Mara reached for her daughter's hand and laced her fingers into a strong clasp. "That's awesome, honey. I do, too, finally."

Cadence hugged Mara. "Joel helped us get it together. He helped us figure out that

God loves us even when we're scared and think no one cares. Joel can't be missing from my quilt when he's such a big part of our lives, can he?"

Mara squeezed Cadence's shoulders. "No, he can't be missing." She wanted to make that a permanent reality in her life, too, but an idea sparked on how to fix the quilt. "I think I have just the right solution."

Cadence stood up. "Okay, what can I do to help?"

"Well, first you're going to need to make some T-shirt transfers again. Then head out to the T-shirt shop and get them ironed on to these leftover quilt blocks."

"On it." She picked up the photos.

Mara sighed as she traced out a new design. Joel really had become part of their lives. Maybe in honoring Cadence's feelings, she could also show Joel that she felt he belonged in their family.

"You so have to see this!" Cadence grabbed Joel's hand and dragged him through the door.

"Whoa, what's up?" He laughed and let her yank him down the hall into Mara's workroom. Mara blinked in surprise at him as they plunged through the entry. "Evidently there's something exciting in here."

"There is?"

"M-o-m." Cadence pointed at the quilt spread out on the table.

Joel whistled. "Wow, that is something. I saw the sketch, but wow." He walked around the table perusing each square, each intricate detail. Louie showed up in a couple of prominent pictures. Joel smiled and touched one. "This is your life. Such a beautiful life, Cadence." He lightly skimmed the beadwork on one block with his fingertips. "There aren't words. Wow!"

Cadence practically purred in pleasure as she stroked the beautiful quilt.

Joel moved toward Mara. She stood up to let him pass, but he caught her around the waist. "Mara," he turned her to look at him, "your quilt is almost as beautiful as you are."

"Thank you." She smiled and lifted her lips up to him for a light kiss.

"Geez, guys." Cadence made her eyes roll. "Show him, Mom."

"Show me what?"

"The grande finale!" Cadence flipped the quilt to show the backside. Another quilt block was on a panel attached like a giant pocket. "Check it out!"

The eight-by-ten of him in his black tails and Mara in her red gown against a backdrop of the Northern Lights, surrounded by the twinkling white lights of the photographer's archway, held center court to four other snapshots on the large pocket. Each of the three kids posed with Joel in their own photo and a special all-inclusive snow cave photo.

He remembered when each happened. One with Marisa at the hospital cafeteria when the doctor came to tell them Mara could go home. Another picture Cadence took of Toby and Joel in the bleachers after the big basketball game against their rival on Senior Night. Joel remembered the honor he'd felt when Toby asked him to stand in for his parents while Mara was in the hospital for her last night. Cadence made him pose with her in front of the dinosaur bones at the museum before the ball. Then the ice castle. That day would stand out in his memory for years.

"I don't understand why you sewed a pocket on the back?"

Mara reached past him. "Because this isn't any ordinary quilt." She flipped it back over. Then she started at one side and she folded in the quilt lengthwise in thirds.

Cadence took over from the top where she stood. "She sewed in a big pocket for me so I can take it to college and use it as either a quilt or a pillow. The whole thing folds right up," she finished and tucked the material into the pocketed space, "into a quillow." The newly formed pillow had all their smiling faces on the front.

"That is cool! I almost feel part of the family!"

Both ladies glowed.

Mara touched his arm. "Do you think she likes it?" They laughed together.

"Yes, and if she doesn't, I sure do!"

"Oh, no, you don't." Cadence clasped the quillow to her. "She made this one for me. You're going to have to ask her for one of your own, dude."

"I wouldn't dream of taking that one from you. But I might have to do some persuading over here." He tilted his head toward the door. "Cadence, could I have a minute with your mom?"

"You bet." She whisked out of the room hugging her new treasure.

"It seems like she's pretty happy." Joel said as he wrapped his arms around Mara. "I'm honored you added me to the quilt. Surprised and touched, too."

Mara tipped her head up to look into Joel's face. "It seemed to us that you, well, that you were the one who held our family together just as the quillow pocket holds the quilt. We wanted to convey our appreciation. We couldn't have made it through this year without you."

"I wouldn't have wished this year on you for anything."

"Are you kidding? Okay, maybe I'd skip the heart attacks if I could. But God used some pretty rough circumstances to bring us back to him, as you pointed out in the restaurant the other night." She added softly, "And to bring you into our lives."

Joel touched her cheek. "Do you realize you haven't used your go-to phrase?"

"My go-to phrase?"

"When you feel frustrated or you've given up the fight, you don't say yes or no. You say 'fine, fine.' " He mimicked her words and common hand motion of flicking the air. "I haven't heard you say that in a long time now."

"Well, I must not be frustrated any more. And I'm feeling a lot of hope now." She leaned into his arms. "Thank you, Joel, for helping me get back to my art and for holding me accountable to live out God's will in my life."

"You're welcome." He pulled away and turned toward her. "Mara, I have one more suggestion as your coach." His voice took on a serious note. "You may want to pray over it first. If you do, I'll pray with you."

314

"I can't think of anything we haven't covered for the business."

"Neither can I." Joel's eyes were soft.

Mara wracked her brain. "What is it?"

Joel handed her a padded envelope with the Museum of the Rockies logo on it.

"What's this?" She took the package.

"Open it and see." He gave her a mysterious smile.

Mara pulled the flap out and tipped it onto the table. A blue velvet box tumbled out.

Joel picked the box up and opened the lid. He watched her reaction closely.

She gasped. "A sapphire ring?" She looked from the ring, nestled against white velvet, to Joel. "You won the mining adventure? Ah, that's why the bids were so high."

"I didn't win the adventure, Mara." He lifted her hand from her side. "I bid on the ring later. When you saw the mining adventure, you said Montana Yogo sapphires were your favorite stone."

"Joel, it's beautiful." She stared at him mystified. Could this be going where she thought it was going? Her heart lifted higher than the Bridgers.

"My suggestion is . . ." he slipped the ring on her finger, "you marry me."

Mara prayed silent thanks to the Lord.

"Fine, fine." She winked at him and swept her hand like she flicked a flea.

Joel tossed his head back and roared with laughter. "I'll fine, fine you." He gathered her tightly into his arms again.

She looked up into his blue, blue eyes and drowned in the endless big skies of hope and love. "I suppose this means you'll want your own quilt made?"

"Filled with memories of our life together." Joel lowered his lips and kissed her.

A NOTE TO THE READER

Louie is based on our family pet of fourteen years who died of pituitary cancer in Fall 2011. Our vet, Dr. Andy Cross, has prayed with us over every horse, dog, and cat he's treated. I admire how Dr. Cross displays his faith through veterinarian practice and hope the depiction inspires others. The prayer in the book is my best recollection of our prayer over Louie, with our family gathered around. Louie could actually do, and did do, most of the things in the book, including shredding our door while we were on vacation. He had more tricks than I could include, but there wasn't room for the sake of the story. But the avalanche event is loosely based on a recent news story of another heroic Montana dog. I have no doubt our Louie would have done exactly as the story reads, if in the same situation. He really was the Chuck Norris of dogs!

A Healing Heart is set in Bozeman, Montana. Many actual setting places were used to give flavor and ambience to the story including Fairy Lake, the Bridger Mountains, Bridger Bowl Ski Area, Museum of the Rockies, Montana Ale Works, and McKenzie River Pizza. If you vacation in Montana, these are must-see-and-do experiences, and as an author, I thought you'd enjoy seeing them in the book.

The Museum Ball is an actual event. It's held each February, usually before Valentine's Day. This year the ball is on Feb. 9, 2013, though it's not referenced in the book. At the time of writing, the Museum of the Rockies loved the theme idea I proposed for the book. Why the Northern Lights theme? Because 2013 is predicted to have spectacular aurora borealis displays due to the expected solar flare activity. The Museum of the Rockies is home to the Taylor Planetarium. During 2013, Taylor Planetarium will be reopened with new seating, digital shows, and a facelift. How much more perfect could the theme be? They thought so, too. I hope you'll stop in and enjoy a show in the newly designed planetarium. I plan to take my grandsons!

The ice castle originally started as an igloo or ice cave. They're built in extreme weather for protection. My husband, Mike, an Eagle

Scout, actually built one with his troop that was so hot inside they had to take the roof off! But in researching how they are made, I found an amazing ice castle on Youtube, complete with a slide, built by a family in Michigan. I couldn't help myself. I had to put one in *A Healing Heart.* I hope you played on the castle with me as you read, too. With enough people, anyone could create a spectacular ice castle for a winter's fun. Plan a party and send me pictures!

No reference is made to a specific doctor or the hospital name in *A Healing Heart* because the events of the story are fictitious. The hospital in Bozeman is excellent, and I hold it in high regard. The reason I chose to include a misdiagnosis, albeit vague, is the high incidence of misdiagnosis of heart attacks in women, according to research from the American Heart Institute. The Go Red for Women campaign has become a prominent force in educating both women and health care professionals on how heart attacks are presented differently in women than men. I encourage you to discover more about your heart health.

The photo memory quilt can be made many ways from T-shirt transfers to the new material printers. I chose to depict the T-shirt transfers because many people may not own a personal material printer and because this is how our family makes photo memory quilts. All six of our children received one from their grandma upon graduation from high school.

My part was to go through their entire lives' worth of photos and choose those that would be highlighted on the quilt. Let me tell you, that was the hardest part! How do you choose from so many memories? Then I was assigned to create the photo transfers and find a T-shirt shop to iron them on for me. Each quilt is unique and incredible with favorite colors, chosen by the child, and designed by their grandma, with her quilting friends. Additionally, each child in our family receives their life in a scrapbook so the photos are preserved once copied onto the quilt. Their graduation parties were spectacular as all their friends poured over the quilt pictures and scrapbooks.

I'd love to hear from you, see the quilts and ice castles you make, and chat with your book clubs and Bible studies. My website and contact is www.AngelaBreidenbach .com, and you can find me on Facebook at www.facebook.com/AngelaBreidenbachIn spirationalSpeakerAuthor and twitter @ Ang Breidenbach, too.

May you share your talents and heritage

with those you love. May God guide you into the special purpose He knit into your DNA. May you feel fulfilled as you live out God's purpose for your life and change the world.

Angie Breidenbach
February 2012

DISCUSSION QUESTIONS

1. What did the story of Jephthah sacrificing his only daughter to fulfill a promise mean to you? (See Judges 11.)

2. How did (or will) you resolve the conflict of a broken promise?

3. What symptoms does Mara experience that should have alerted her to the first heart attack? (www.GoRedForWomen.org Click on Heart Check UP if you don't know.)

4. What does Louie, the dog, symbolize in *A Healing Heart*?

5. How did you feel about the concept of prayer when Louie died?

6. What do you understand, in Genesis 1:26-28, of God's intent for mankind to

be in charge of the animals?

7. Would you be able to trust someone like Joel? Why or why not?

8. What do you think of Joel's nickname for God?

9. Do you have names for God other than the formal biblical names? Share them and what they mean.

10. What did you think of the ice castle's part in the way Mara's family created a memorial for their dad and dog?

11. Why do men need to be under the authority of God and submit to the authority of another man such as Joel's coach, Rich?

12. Read Ecclesiastes 2:11. How does it apply to Mara's refusal to delegate duties?

13. Mara's refusal to delegate could be seen as a psychological form of hoarding. What steps can you take to either change the habit of hoarding duties or help someone else begin to delegate?

14. How do you pass on heritage and stories to your children and younger family members?

15. Is there something you'd like to learn from an older relative about your family, heritage, or a skill?

16. In what way did Mrs. Calder and the women from Mara's church act as the hands of God on earth?

17. Who reached out first, the women from church or Mara? What does this suggest to us?

18. Mara has a business coach. What do you know about business, life, or other professional coaches?

19. What kind of a coach might you like to have? Why?

20. How did you see forgiveness change lives in *A Healing Heart*?

21. What do you think will happen in the future for Mara and Joel?